*Find out who you are
and do it on purpose.*

–Dolly Parton

MYSTERIES *of* LANCASTER COUNTY

Another's Treasure
Garage Sale Secret
An Unbroken Circle
Mixed Signals

MIXED SIGNALS

MYSTERIES *of* LANCASTER COUNTY

Beth Adams

Guideposts

New York

MIXED SIGNALS

CHAPTER ONE

Elizabeth Classen watched as the barns and farmhouses rolled by through the glass. These roads were as familiar to her as her own skin, and she loved seeing the countryside go past. Lights were coming on inside the homes, shining through windows with a warm glow, and quiet was settling over the fields and barnyards as Amish farmers led their horses inside for the night. She loved the familiar rhythm of it. But with each field and farm that passed, she was that much closer to the night ending. A part of her dreaded reaching home.

She glanced over at John. His mouth curled up in just a hint of a smile as he drove. John had invited her to join him at a Lancaster Symphony concert in a park in Lancaster. It had been a nice evening, and they'd had great conversation and lots of laughs, and now he was driving her home. They sat in comfortable silence. She loved that he didn't feel the need to fill the quiet with senseless chatter. There was something wonderful about a friend you could be quiet with. A *friend,* she reminded herself. Nothing more.

They were about to pass the Hostetler farm, which meant they were just a few miles from the family farmhouse she now shared with her two sisters. But as John made a right turn onto the rural road that led over the creek and toward her home, something caught her eye.

She narrowed her eyes. "What is that?"

John slowed the car. "I have no idea."

The long country road stretched out before them, gathering shadows as the summer evening turned into night. Cornfields ran as far as the eye could see on both sides of the road, and the rolling hills of the quiet Pennsylvania countryside gave the whole scene a peaceful, wholesome feel.

"It's some kind of light," Elizabeth said, gazing down the road. What in the world? It looked like the light was coming from the ground, and it was blinking on and off.

"Almost like a strobe light," John confirmed.

"But it's coming from the ditch." As they got closer, Elizabeth could see more clearly that the blinking white light was coming from some kind of device by the side of the road. But what was it, and why was it there? The sky was a deep royal blue, edging toward black, and the soft breeze rustled the dark cornstalks. As night settled in, the blinking white light seemed eerily out of place.

John slowed the car to a stop and then put it in PARK. "Stay here," he said, unbuckling his seat belt. But Elizabeth pushed open her door and stepped out after him. John Marks might be a member of the East Lampeter police force, but Elizabeth wasn't afraid of a little light. She stepped out of the car onto the soft grassy shoulder and followed just a few steps behind him as he moved toward the strobe's source. It had been a wet week, and the ground felt spongy underneath her feet.

"It's a phone," John said, crouching down. Elizabeth came up beside him and saw that he was right. An iPhone lay face-down on the slope of the culvert, blinking a bright white light on and off rapidly from the camera lens. She stepped forward and reached for it, and John put his arm out to steady her as she bent over the sloping dirt side of the ditch.

"Who would leave a phone by the side of the road?" Elizabeth picked up the phone and straightened up. "Especially one that looks as new as this one." She turned it over in her hands. It looked to be a newer model iPhone and had a sparkly pink case. These things were expensive.

John didn't say anything for a moment but looked around, surveying the area.

"Is anyone out there?" he called, looking off into the rows of cornstalks. They were only about waist high but densely planted and could easily hide a crouching person, Elizabeth thought with a shiver. But the only answer was the hum of cicadas.

John turned around in a circle, looking at the ground. His headlights illuminated a small patch of dirt at the side of the road, and John walked over now to look.

"What do you see?" Elizabeth asked.

"Tire marks," John said, nudging the soft earth with his toe. "Someone peeled out of here in a hurry."

"And left their phone behind," Elizabeth added.

"Yes." John nodded. "Though I'm guessing they didn't intend to do that."

"I'm sure you're right." People these days were all but surgically attached to their phones. She couldn't imagine someone would leave it behind on purpose. She touched the smooth round button at the bottom of the phone's face, and the screen lit up, showing a dark field with a white disk in the middle.

"And I'm sure whoever owns this phone is missing it. So how do we figure out who to return it to?"

John didn't answer for a moment. He studied the phone, which was still blinking a light on and off in some kind of pattern.

"What is it?" Elizabeth prodded.

There was a strange look on John's face, and he was staring off into the cornfield once again.

"I'm just trying to figure out what happened here," he said, and he reached his hand out, silently asking her to hand him the phone. Elizabeth gave it to him, and he tapped the circle on the screen so the light turned off.

"People don't often just drive away and leave their phones behind," Elizabeth said.

John waited a moment before answering. The rising moon sat low and large in the sky, casting a silvery light over everything. He tapped the screen again, but a lock screen came up, and John was prompted to type in a passcode to access the phone.

"That's true, but I think it's more than that," John said. He was turning in a slow circle again, looking carefully in every direction. He took a few steps, and Elizabeth saw that he was moving toward the bridge that ran over the small creek a hundred feet or so down the road. Elizabeth followed behind him and watched as he used the light on his own cell phone to illuminate the area under the bridge and along the creek bed.

"What is it?" Elizabeth asked again. Something was putting him on high alert.

"I don't see anything here," he said, turning back toward the car.

"What were you looking for?" she asked, coming up alongside him as he turned again, searching in the distance.

"I'm not sure," he said.

Elizabeth felt frustration rise up in her. Was he being purposefully obtuse? What wasn't he saying?

"John." She tried to keep her voice calm and level, even as a bit of fear began to thread through her. "What's going on?"

John stopped next to the spot where they'd found the phone. He let out a long, deep breath.

"I'm not sure," he finally repeated. "Maybe nothing. But I worry something bad might have happened here."

She had started to feel the same way herself, and the way he was acting wasn't helping. But she tried to keep calm. "Why do you say that?"

"You know that flashing light that attracted us here in the first place?"

She nodded.

"It wasn't just blinking a random pattern. It was Morse code for SOS."

CHAPTER TWO

Elizabeth remained unsettled the rest of the drive back to the Classen farm. She held the phone on her lap, trying to touch it as little as possible in case the police needed to dust it for fingerprints. She wished now she hadn't picked it up at all. Had she messed up whatever evidence was there? But John *was* the police, and he had touched it too. He would know what to do, she tried to convince herself. Still, she worried.

When they pulled up in front of the farmhouse, John came around the passenger side of the car and opened her door while she gathered her purse. It felt silly—she was a grown woman who could certainly open her own door—but it was also kind of sweet. The night air was warm and soft, and the cicadas hummed. The old barn—now the secondhand and gift store she ran with her two sisters—stood in shadows across the yard. John walked her up the steps of the front porch to the door, and she pushed it open and ushered him inside.

"Hello!" Martha called from the kitchen. It smelled like she was baking. "In here."

"Hi there," Elizabeth said. She set her purse down and led John down the hallway to the kitchen. Martha was surrounded by bowls and had a streak of flour on her cheek. She was stirring chocolate chips into a bowl of batter. Loaves of chocolate zucchini bread were cooling on wire racks on the far side of the counter. Yum. The best way to serve vegetables was to add chocolate to them, Elizabeth had always thought. Martha baked the fresh goodies they sold in Secondhand Blessings, and she had clearly gotten the baking for the store out of the way before turning to the more fun baking. Martha's son Craig and his family were set to arrive tomorrow morning for a visit, and Martha had been stocking up on the kids' favorite foods for days.

"Hi, John," Martha said, smiling as Elizabeth led him into the room. "How was your evening?"

"The concert was really nice," Elizabeth said. She didn't know much about classical music, but she'd recognized the *1812 Overture*, and that was fun.

"Very well done," John added.

"But..." Martha stopped stirring and looked at Elizabeth, and then back at John. Martha had been very much in favor of Elizabeth's growing friendship with John, and Elizabeth knew she was eager to hear the details of their night. But after the way it had all ended, she was unsettled, and Martha had obviously picked up on that.

"But something strange happened on the way home," Elizabeth said.

John set the phone on the counter and excused himself to call down to the station and report what had happened. He stepped out onto the back steps and into the yard while Elizabeth quickly explained. While she was talking, her youngest sister, Mary, came in from the living room holding a thick paperback book Elizabeth could have sworn had been for sale in the shop this afternoon. Mary had no doubt been reading and overheard. Like her sisters, she could never resist a mystery. She listened as Elizabeth explained about the blinking light and how they thought someone had been trying to call for help. She reminded them that John was a navy veteran, which explained how he'd recognized the distress signal. Mary set her book on the counter and settled into one of the barstools at the counter.

"Well, I think it's fair to say this someone was probably a woman," Martha said, indicating the glittery pink case around the phone.

"You're probably right about that," Elizabeth said.

"I assume the phone has a passcode?" Mary asked.

Elizabeth nodded. "If we could get into the phone, we might be able to figure out who it belongs to, but I'm not sure how to guess the passcode."

"Aren't there some really common passcodes?" Martha asked. "I thought I read somewhere that there are a few that are really popular."

"I read that too," Elizabeth said. "We could try some of those, but I'm afraid to touch it too much until John decides if he wants to dust it for fingerprints."

"Good point," Mary said.

For a moment, no one spoke, but they all looked at the phone, trying to make sense of it. Who did it belong to? What had happened to her?

"Do you guys remember Amber Barber?" Mary finally asked.

Martha let out a long breath. "I was thinking about her too."

Elizabeth's mind had gone to that as well, but she tried to force herself to think rationally. The name brought back such visceral memories, so much buried fear and anxiety.

"They never found out what happened to her, did they?" Mary asked.

"No, they didn't," Elizabeth confirmed. No one needed to remind them of the story that had haunted the community for years. Amber Barber had only been fourteen the day she disappeared. She'd gone to visit at a neighboring farm after school that October day, and she was last seen leaving her friend's driveway about suppertime on her bike. The ride was only a mile along a straight country road, but Amber had never made it home, and her bike was found abandoned in a cornfield five miles away. She had vanished, and though the police and the whole community searched for months, no trace of her was ever found. Elizabeth had been eighteen when it happened, and she remembered the grief and terror that had gripped the community in the years following the disappearance. No one had believed that something like that could happen here in rural Pennsylvania, surrounded by cornfields and Amish buggies. For years afterwards, parents were fearful of letting their children go anywhere alone. Elizabeth still thought about Amber whenever she drove past the spot where the poor girl vanished.

"This can't be the same sort of thing, can it?" Mary asked.

"Of course not," Martha said, with a bit too much force.

"Let's not jump to conclusions," Elizabeth said. "We don't know who the phone belongs to, or what happened to her."

"But it *is* a girl," Mary said, pointing to the pink case.

"I think that's very likely," Elizabeth said. "And hopefully it won't be hard to figure out who that girl is."

The back door opened, and John stepped back in, holding his cell phone in one hand and a small black case in the other.

"Any news?" Elizabeth asked.

"There have been no missing person reports filed." He set the case on the counter. "And no reports of a missing or stolen phone."

"Maybe that's a good thing," Mary said, ever the optimist. "Maybe that means there's not really anything wrong. That someone simply dropped her phone and will come back to look for it."

"Maybe..." Elizabeth met John's eye. They both wanted to believe that, but neither did.

"Well, just in case, I brought in my fingerprint kit," John said. He opened the snaps on the black plastic case.

"Wait. You're driving your personal car, not a police car," Elizabeth said. "Do you just carry one of these things around with you all the time?"

John shrugged as he opened the case and pulled out a small bottle of black powder. "I'm never really off duty. It doesn't take up much space in the trunk."

Elizabeth could see that her sisters were as impressed as she was. They watched as he reached for the phone and then used a small brush from the kit to spread the powder over the face and back of the phone. Elizabeth had seen this done on crime shows on television, but she'd never seen it happen in real life.

"Any luck?" Martha asked.

"Not really," John said slowly. "There are lots of partials but not any that look like they would be much use."

"I shouldn't have touched it," Elizabeth said.

"I held it too," John said. "And given how often most people touch their phones, it was very unlikely there would be any full or even clear partial prints anyway. But I had to try, just in case."

He didn't say in case of what, but Elizabeth understood. In case there had been foul play involved and there was a clue on the phone. He pulled a small packet out of the kit, removed a moist towelette from it, and wiped the phone to clean off the black powder.

"I guess we'll have to wait and see if anyone reports it missing," John said. "Or if the owner uses location services to figure out where it is."

"Uses what now?" Elizabeth had a cell phone, but she wasn't exactly up on all the features and technology behind it.

"Location services. Like Find My iPhone," Mary said. "If you lose your phone, you can log into the cloud from your computer or another connected device and find its location."

"Into the cloud?" Elizabeth repeated. She looked from Mary to John and back again.

"Don't worry about the details. What she means is that the owner of this phone is probably looking for it and may very well be able to figure out where it is," Martha said.

"Let's hope so," Elizabeth said. "And let's hope she's all right."

"I'm sure it will all work out, and we're worried for no reason," Mary said.

As much as Elizabeth wanted to believe her, she couldn't let go of the unsettled feeling in her gut.

That night, Elizabeth plugged in her own cell phone in the living room to charge and then headed up to bed. John had stayed long enough to sample one of Martha's fresh-baked chocolate chip cookies, and the conversation had moved on from the phone and its missing owner to the upcoming county fair, and then to Martha talking about her grandchildren who were coming the next day. But even as the conversation flowed, Elizabeth hadn't been able to shake the anxious thoughts that had settled over her. She couldn't believe, as Mary suggested, that the phone had been left there innocently. Just an accident, and someone would come back for it soon. Elizabeth couldn't help believing there was more to it than that.

Elizabeth sighed and changed into her thin cotton night-gown. Maybe everything would look better in the morning. Maybe she'd be thinking more clearly, and a perfectly logical explanation would present itself. A light breeze ruffled the curtain through the open window. This old house didn't have central air. Elizabeth had threatened to have it installed many times over the years, but Mama couldn't imagine spending that much on something they would only use a few months a year at most. Elizabeth realized that she could go ahead and have it installed now that her parents were gone, but she wasn't sure if she wanted to. There were window units that they dragged out of the basement when the dog days of summer got to be unbearable, and she'd had one running in her room last night, but the house was situated on a rise, and the windows on two sides of the room caught a nice breeze.

Besides, they couldn't spend the money on something optional right now anyway, Elizabeth realized. She glanced at the corner of the room, where the floral wallpaper had been peeled away in large strips. The plaster underneath bloomed with a brown stain, a remnant of a powerful thunderstorm a few nights ago that had torn some shingles off the roof and led to a leak in the ceiling and down her wall. They'd peeled the wallpaper off, hoping to salvage the plaster underneath, but it had been soggy for a few days, and Elizabeth was fairly certain it would need to be replaced. She knew she should be grateful that her bedroom was the only part of the house that had been damaged, but right now it just seemed like a big hassle.

"Think of it as an opportunity."

Elizabeth jumped a bit and whirled around. "Mary! I didn't hear you come in."

"Sorry, I didn't mean to scare you. I just came to make sure you were doing okay." Mary came up next to Elizabeth and snaked her arm around her back. Elizabeth leaned in against her younger sister. The smell of her rose-scented lotion was so familiar. "I could tell you were a little shaken up by what happened tonight."

"You're right." Elizabeth nodded. "I was. I don't know what happened out there, but I can't help thinking someone is in trouble."

"Well, if they are, the police will help them," Mary said.

Elizabeth didn't say anything.

"I take that silence to mean you won't be leaving this one to the police," Mary said.

"How can I? I found the phone. Of course I want to find out what happened to the girl."

"Then I'll do whatever I can to help," Mary said.

Elizabeth appreciated it, though it had never really been a question. She'd known her sisters would help her, no matter what.

"And I still think it's an opportunity," Mary said, gesturing toward the water damage.

"I think of it more as a big mess," Elizabeth said.

"Seriously, though. When was the last time you redecorated in here?" Mary looked around the room, which was furnished with an antique iron bedstead topped with an heirloom quilt, the same simple wooden dresser that Elizabeth had used in high school, and an oak secretary desk she'd bought at an antique store years ago. Elizabeth loved the simple front and the wide drawers beneath.

"Redecorate?" Elizabeth looked around the room. "Why?"

Mary pursed her lips, and her forehead wrinkled. Then, after a short pause, she said, "Now, there's nothing wrong with the room. But it couldn't hurt to freshen things up a bit, could it?"

This had been Elizabeth's childhood bedroom, and she'd settled into it again when she'd moved home more than ten years ago. She'd selected the wallpaper and most of the furnishings back in high school. It was so familiar that she couldn't see it with fresh eyes, but she tried to see what Mary saw. The muslin curtains did look sort of yellowed, she had to admit.

And maybe a bit tattered down there at the bottom, if she was honest. And the brass light fixture on the ceiling could use a good cleaning. Now that she thought about it, she hadn't seen one like it in years. Maybe she could stand to swap it out for something that gave off more light. The braided rug beside the bed was looking rattier than she'd realized.

"You'll have to peel off the wallpaper anyway," Mary said gently.

"I don't know. I thought I might be able to find a roll of that pattern somewhere." Elizabeth loved the print of large pink and white cabbage roses and tender green leaves. It was elegant, but simple and beautiful.

Mary paused before saying, "Even if you did, it wouldn't match the paper that's been on the walls for years."

Elizabeth narrowed her eyes, and she saw what Mary was getting at. The wallpaper did look dingy. The white roses were more tan, and the background, which used to be a beautiful robin's-egg blue, was more of a seafoam now.

"I guess you're right," she said. "But what would I replace it with?"

"I'm sure we could find something you love," Mary said. "We'll repaint the walls, get you some new linens and a throw pillow or two, maybe upgrade the furniture. Maybe give the mantel a nice coat of white paint. It would brighten things up so much."

"Paint the mantel?" One of Elizabeth's favorite features of the room was the old fireplace with the original wooden mantel. It was carved cherry, and it was a beautiful bronze color. Or, it had been, Elizabeth realized. It had turned into a dingy gray, now that she was looking at it carefully. But still. "You can't paint wood." As far as she was concerned, it was a sin to cover up richly grained wood with boring old paint.

"You can, though," Mary said with a smile. "You can do whatever you want. It's your room, and there's no one here to tell you not to."

"I don't know."

But Elizabeth knew that Mary was right—she had to tear down the wallpaper, in any case. Maybe this was the right time to make some other changes. It had been decades. While she'd been caring for Mama, she hadn't even thought about making changes, but now that things were different—now that Martha and Mary had moved back home, and they were all running the shop together—maybe it was time to make a change. But how?

"I wouldn't even know where to start," Elizabeth said.

"I'll help you," Mary said. "It'll be fun. We can look at some magazines and see what kind of styles you like, and then we can go from there."

"I like this style," Elizabeth said, gesturing at the simple, familiar furnishings. What was wrong with the things she had? It was all solid, well-made furniture, and if it was a little plainer than her sister would prefer, so what? Simplicity was always in fashion. Wasn't it?

"Well, yes," Mary said. "But there are lots of fun ways to make it look a little...more stylish. You'll see. This will be exciting."

"Sure," Elizabeth said. "Okay." She wasn't sure she shared her sister's excitement, but she guessed Mary was right. It was probably past time to make some changes, and she had to replace the ruined wallpaper anyway. And Mary was an artist. She had a good eye. With her help, this wouldn't be so painful. Elizabeth tried to make her voice sound as enthusiastic as Mary's, but she wasn't sure she managed it. "This will be fun."

CHAPTER THREE

Elizabeth was sitting at the dining table when Martha came downstairs Saturday morning. A metal fan resting in the corner of the room stirred the air lazily, but it was already clear it was going to be hot today. Pal, their eight-year-old border collie, was sleeping at Elizabeth's feet.

"Good morning," Martha called as she stepped into the kitchen. Elizabeth looked up from the laptop on the table in front of her. Martha headed straight for the coffee maker.

"Hi there. Did you sleep all right?"

Martha opened the lid and set a filter inside. "I slept okay." Truthfully, it had taken her a long time to fall asleep, and she'd woken several times in the night. She knew it was silly, but she'd felt like a kid on Christmas Eve. Her grandkids were coming today! Well, two of them, anyway. At thirteen, Kevin was her oldest grandchild, and as the first, he would always have a special place in her heart. Dylan was ten and hilarious. And Craig was coming, of course, and his wife, Molly. Martha opened the glass jar that held the ground coffee and started to scoop it into the machine. She was excited to see Craig and Molly and to catch up on their lives, but if she were honest, most of all she really couldn't wait to hug those grandkids. People had warned her that she would love her grandchildren with a fierce kind of love she'd never known before, but she had still been surprised by how it felt to hold those babies for the first time. It wasn't the same sort of powerful, primal love she'd felt for her children; it was just as strong, but different, somehow.

"You slept so well you're using twice the normal amount of coffee?" Elizabeth was smiling at her.

Martha looked down and realized there was an abnormally large amount of ground coffee in the filter basket. "It's possible that my brain might be elsewhere this morning." She laughed and scooped some of the coffee back into the jar.

"You're excited."

"I guess I am." Butterscotch, their marmalade tabby, brushed his back against her legs.

"Of course you are. What time do they arrive?"

"The flight is supposed to land in Harrisburg at ten. They're renting a car, and Craig said they'd call when they got close." The drive took about an hour, so she wouldn't expect them to arrive before eleven at the earliest. The trip from Kansas was long, and they'd no doubt be tired and hungry by the time they arrived, so Martha was planning to have meat loaf and mashed potatoes and homemade biscuits—Craig's favorite—for dinner tonight. After she ate breakfast and had some coffee, Martha would head to the store to load up on groceries. She looked down at the coffee and pressed the red button, and the machine gurgled as it started to heat the water. Martha turned to Elizabeth.

"What are you working on?" It was rare to see her older sister hunched over a laptop like that. Of the three of them, she was the least tech savvy.

"Mary said last night that there are some very common passwords, so I wanted to see if I could figure out what they were."

"You're hoping to help the police unlock the phone you found." Martha understood immediately. They all knew that if they could get into the phone, it probably wouldn't be hard to identify the owner. Call records, contacts, social media accounts, and photos would all provide clues that should lead them very quickly to the identity of the woman who owned it. "Of course you are."

Elizabeth was so tenderhearted. She'd probably been up half the night worrying about the girl who'd left the phone behind. The disappearance of Amber Barber all those years ago had affected all of them deeply, and Martha could see that Elizabeth was afraid the kidnapper had struck again. John had taken the phone with him last night, but Elizabeth was still clearly thinking about it and what its presence at the side of the road meant. "Has there been any update? Any clue of what happened to the owner?"

"Not that I know of, but I haven't heard from John, and it's still too early to give him a call to see."

The rich, earthy aroma of coffee began to fill the kitchen. Martha opened the bread drawer and pulled out a plastic bag of blueberry scones she'd made yesterday. She grabbed a scone and took a bite, not even bothering to heat it up or add butter. "So what have you found?"

"According to this page I found, the most common iPhone password is 1234."

"That's not very creative." Butterscotch wound his way around Martha's legs and scraped the side of his face against the edge of the counter.

"It's hard to believe people really use that one," Elizabeth agreed. "So that's obviously the first code I'd suggest they try to use to unlock the phone. The next most common is 0000."

"Seriously?" Martha couldn't believe it. "Are people just asking for their phones to be broken into?" She set the scone down, walked to the pantry, and pulled out the bag of cat food. Butterscotch meowed loudly and led Martha toward his food dish. Pal lifted his head at the sound and then lowered it again and closed his eyes.

"I guess a lot of people don't take security all that seriously," Elizabeth said. "After that, it's 2580—four numbers in a line down the screen—and then 1111 and 5555."

"I guess the good news is, they'll be able to unlock that phone and find out who it belongs to if the owner picked one of those passcodes," Martha said. She dumped some food in the cat's bowl, and he started eating greedily. She set the food back on the shelf, closed the pantry door, and then took another bite of the scone. She really should heat it up, but she was in too much of a hurry. "Maybe John already has, in fact."

"Let's hope so. I'll give him a call in a little while," Elizabeth said. "In the meantime, I'll go feed the animals." She closed the lid of her laptop and sighed.

"Sounds good," Martha said. They didn't have a large farm—just a few goats and some chickens for fresh eggs, but they did need to be fed and watered each morning and evening, and the sisters all pitched in. "I'm going to run to the grocery store. Is there anything you want to add to the list?" She pointed to the notepad that sat on the counter.

"Not that I can think of," Elizabeth said.

"Okay. I'll get going then." Martha put the last of the scone in her mouth and brushed her fingers together over the sink. The earlier she got to the store, the less crowded it was, and the more efficient her shopping could be.

A few minutes later, she was driving down the country roads headed toward Lancaster. Martha had a talk-radio station playing, but her mind was mostly focused on adding things to her list as she thought of them. She should get bagels, she thought. Last time her grandchildren had visited her, Kevin had ordered a bagel when they went out to breakfast. And cream cheese. She had to remember bagels and cream cheese. But then, up ahead, she saw something. By the side of the road.

Was that a car?

Martha slowed as she approached. It was a car—a small black sporty two-door that looked like it had seen better days. A Camaro. But what was it doing parked at the side of the road? Martha slowed to a crawl and looked toward the car. There was no one inside. No one around.

It was probably nothing, she told herself. Just a farmer who had come out to check on his soybeans. But why wouldn't he take his tractor out, then? People didn't just leave cars abandoned by the side of the road around here.

But just because it was here didn't necessarily mean it was abandoned, did it? There was no reason to think that it was. She was letting Elizabeth's excitement over the phone she'd found make her think everything was suspicious. There was no doubt a perfectly normal—and not at all sinister—explanation. Parking a car by the road was not a crime.

In her rearview mirror, she saw an Amish buggy coming up the road toward her, the horses' hooves making the familiar clip-clopping sound as they hit the pavement. Martha put her foot on the gas and accelerated. She needed to just keep focused on her tasks. There was a lot to get done before Craig and the grandkids arrived.

It was more than an hour later, her car loaded up with groceries, when Martha turned down the same road and saw the car still parked in the same spot. Martha slowed again. There was no reason to think that anything about this was suspicious, she reminded herself. But still, she found herself braking to a stop and climbing out. It couldn't hurt anything just to take a look, she rationalized as she walked toward the car. Just to make sure there was nothing strange going on.

She approached the car and put her hand on the hood. The engine was cold. Then she stepped up to the passenger-side window, took a deep breath, and peered inside the car. There was no one inside—not that she'd expected there would be. A strange sense of relief coursed through her. She realized that a small part of her had been fearing she would find some gruesome crime scene. She shook her head. She was too rational for flights of fancy like that. It just looked like a normal car. A messy car, but a normal one. There were fast-food wrappers on the floor and CD cases and papers strewn across the back seat. And on the passenger seat, there were more papers. Maps, printouts, receipts—

Wait. Martha squinted to make sure she was seeing this right. That was a receipt from Secondhand Blessings. She tried to make out the small letters on the cash register receipt. It was from July 7. That was last Saturday, Martha realized. One week ago. And the receipt was for...linens, she thought it said. Whenever they rang up a sale in the store, the register asked them to assign a category to the purchase. Linens was a broad category that included bedding, towels, tablecloths... pretty much anything made of fabric that wasn't clothes. Martha thought about this for a moment and realized she and her sisters could probably piece together a list of the people who had bought linens last Saturday. But why? What good would that do? Martha shook her head. There was nothing wrong here. No crime. No reason to be poking around peering into cars by the side of the road.

Someone had probably had engine trouble, she thought as she walked back toward her car. There was no mystery here. But still, she couldn't stop herself from taking out her phone and snapping a picture of the car, being sure to get a clear shot of the license plate, before climbing into her car and heading back toward home. There was a lot to get done today. Best to forget about this nonsense and get ready for—she felt a thrill go through her—her grandkids to arrive.

Mary crossed the yard and got the shop ready for the day— stocking the register, turning on the air conditioner and fans—a little before opening time. She loved this shop, with its

Amish-made oak shelves brimming with one-of-a-kind pieces and the quilts and needlework adorning the walls. It felt warm and homey, and the high-pitched ceiling and the wooden walls that reminded their customers it was a barn gave the whole space charm and character. She drank another cup of coffee as she worked. It would no doubt be a busy day, and she had slept poorly, her mind circling around the story of Amber Barber, wondering what had become of her and whether the girl who had lost her phone last night had met a similar fate. Now, in the light of day, she tried to think about happier things, but she couldn't entirely shake her distress.

She looked up as someone walked in the shop door. Several someones, in fact.

"Hello there," she called out as Della Bradford, Nancy VanSlyke, Beverly Stout, and Linda Martin came in. The women were regulars who scoured estate sales and garage sales during the week and often brought the best of what they found to the shop so the Classen sisters could sell it on consignment.

"Hi, Mary," Beverly called, carrying a large cardboard box in her arms. Both Della and Linda carried shopping bags.

"It looks like you ladies have had a busy week," Mary said. Getting to know the regulars was one of the many blessings about moving back to Bird-in-Hand. In the short time since she and Martha had moved home to live with Elizabeth and reopen the shop their parents had run for years, these ladies had become more than customers—they'd become friends. "What did you bring me?"

"We found some fun things," Nancy said. Her brown hair was threaded with gray, and she moved with an easy grace. She set the tote bag she was carrying on the counter and pulled out a set of ivory dominoes, a tarnished silver ladle, and an intricately worked lace doily.

"This is beautiful." Mary pulled the set of dominoes closer to her and examined them. "This set is old."

"It has to be, right?" Nancy said. "I don't know how old, but I thought it was pretty."

"It is." Mary set the dominoes aside and reached for the ladle. She didn't recognize the pattern, but that wouldn't be hard to find out. She turned the piece over and found the letters *EPNS* in tiny letters on the back of the handle. Electroplated nickel silver. Silver plate, then. Still beautiful but not nearly as valuable as if the piece had been sterling.

"You got that at the Watson estate sale, right?" Della asked. Nancy nodded.

"They had some nice things." Della pulled a long camel-colored wool coat, well-made and exquisitely tailored, out of her bag. "This is from the fifties, I think. There's a bit of moth damage on one of the cuffs, but otherwise it's in very good shape." There was a fur collar, and the buttons were stamped brass.

"It's beautiful." Mary took the coat and examined it. As Della had said, there were a few tiny moth holes along the edge of one of the sleeves, but overall it was very nice. Many of the items they sold in the store were simple, everyday useful things—gently used pots and pans, previously owned electronics and clothes, books and art that still had the power to brighten someone's day. But Mary's favorites were the things that had a little history, a story that begged to be uncovered and told.

Several weeks back, Della had brought in a silver teapot that was not only beautiful but turned out to be very valuable. Mary now fingered the finely spun wool of the coat, wondering about the woman who had worn it, what she was like, where she had worn such a beautiful coat around these parts. People in this area were less formal than this. Then again, things were different back in the fifties; everyone seemed to dress more carefully then. None of this yoga-pants-as-everyday-clothing craze. Maybe this coat belonged to a farmer's wife who'd lived in a big city and hated being trapped on a farm in the middle of the Pennsylvania countryside. Or maybe it belonged to a woman whose sweetheart had been killed in World War II, who kept his letters tucked into the pockets, who—

"Mary?" Della was looking at her, her head cocked to one side.

"Sorry." Mary felt a flush creep up her cheeks. "I'll take it. It's a beautiful coat."

After she'd worked out pricing on the items Della and Nancy had brought in, Beverly opened her bag. She pulled out a set of decorative Christmas plates—charming, and easy to resell, but not worth much—and a large collection of nicely spun wool yarn. It was high-quality material, and dyed in beautiful bright colors.

"I guess Mrs. Watson was a knitter," Beverly said with a shrug. "There was a bunch of synthetic yarn and some cotton as well, but I only took the wool."

"That's wise," Mary said. They probably could have sold the cheaper yarn, but it would have been for such a low price that it hardly seemed worth the effort. "This is nice."

"I'm glad you think so. But look at this." Beverly's bangle bracelets clanged together as she reached into the bag and pulled out a framed piece of embroidery. Mary took the edges of the frame and studied it.

"Oh, wow." It was exquisite. Mary quickly recognized it as a sampler—needlework done by a young girl to show off her stitching skills. They had several hanging on the walls, but none as old or as beautiful as this. Samplers were commonly made in the nineteenth and early twentieth centuries, when skill at stitching and embroidery were counted among the highest virtues a young girl could possess. They were still quite common in the Amish community that surrounded Bird-in-Hand, though Mary could see quickly that this was made by an *Englisch* girl, not an Amish one. This one was much more elaborately designed and intricately decorated than a typical Amish sampler, which focused more on showing off simple skill with the needle than intricate patterns and motifs. This sampler had a detailed scalloped border in peach and green thread, and a row of flowers connected to a vine ran just inside that. The flowers were worked in shades of peach and green, and another border, this time deep blue, ran just inside that. At the top of the border-framed section was the alphabet, carefully stitched in uppercase cursive letters. Underneath that, the alphabet was repeated in uppercase block letters and then in lowercase block letters. The creator of this piece had been showing off how neatly and beautifully she could make letters of all types, Mary knew.

Beneath the alphabets, there was a picture of a two-story house with a hipped roof and big windows done in a red-brick color next to a weeping willow tree. It was a charming house—was it where the girl had lived? Beneath the house, she'd worked a Bible verse in carefully cross-stitched letters: *Remember now thy Creator in the days of thy youth, while the evil days come not, nor the years draw nigh, when thou shalt say, I have no pleasure in them.* Mary recognized the verse from Ecclesiastes.

At the very bottom of the sampler was her name: *Frances Louisa Hartman, in the twelfth year of her age.* Beneath that, she'd stitched *Lancaster, Pennsylvania,* and then *April 2, 1883.*

"This is beautiful," Mary said.

"This is my favorite part," Nancy said, pointing to a black dot after the 3 in 1883. "Look closely."

Mary leaned in and squinted and saw that the block dot had eight thin lines coming off it. It almost looked like a—

"She made a spider!" Della laughed. "Look at that!"

It was indeed a spider. A tiny black spider. Mary had to laugh. This beautiful piece was done in such delicate feminine colors, and then the girl had gone and added a spider.

"It's small enough that you really have to look closely to see it," Beverly said. "I bet she did that on purpose, so she didn't get in trouble."

"But why do you think she added a spider?" Mary asked.

"Maybe she was a tomboy," Linda said. "And this was her tiny act of rebellion."

"Maybe she was a dark soul who would have been a goth if she'd been born today," Beverly added.

"Maybe she didn't add it. Maybe someone else did that at some later point," Nancy said.

Mary hadn't thought about that. Was there any way to tell? She was hardly an expert on stitching. All she knew was that the piece was beautiful, and the small, discreet spider made her curious. Had Frances added it, and when, and why? She loved the idea that this had been a tiny act of rebellion—a bit of spunk shown in an otherwise proper young lady. But was there any way to know?

"In any case, it's really beautiful," Nancy said.

"It's in good shape," Della said. "A little yellowed, but you'd expect that with something this old."

Mary looked up at Beverly. "Are you sure you want to part with it?" It was such a piece of history.

"Honey, if I kept every beautiful thing I found at estate sales, my house would be filled to the brim, and there would be no room left for my husband. For the sake of my marriage, please take it and find it a good home."

"I'm sure we'll be able to do that." Mary set the sampler down and then went through the other treasures Nancy had brought in. After they'd all agreed on pricing, the four women went out together, chatting about stopping in at Greta's Coffeehouse to get lattes before heading out to hit the day's sales.

Mary recorded the new items in their inventory register and affixed prices to them, but as she went to display the sampler, she decided to sit with it for a while. She was drawn to it for reasons that didn't make sense to her. Maybe it was that spider—that tiny, unexpected bit of personality that made this piece stand out. Maybe it was because her own middle name was Frances. But she felt a connection to the girl, whoever she was.

Should she keep it? But, like Beverly, if she kept every beautiful piece that came through their doors, there would be no room left for anything else in their home. And the last time she'd held on to an item meant for sale, it had caused all kinds of trouble, including Della's disappearance. No, it wasn't a desire to own it that had gripped Mary.

She was curious though. Who was Frances Louise Hartman? What had her life been like? She would have been born not too long after the end of the Civil War. She'd lived close to here, in Lancaster. What had Lancaster been like? Mary tried to picture the city, with its tall buildings, as it would have been then. It probably would have been mostly brick and wooden storefronts and houses, she guessed. Had Frances lived in the city itself? Or in the countryside that surrounded the town?

She'd been twelve when she'd completed this, and judging by the fine workmanship, she'd had plenty of practice with a needle. Mary imagined she spent her days churning butter and gathering eggs and sweeping with a rustic broom. Or maybe sitting on velvet settees under stained glass lampshades, walls draped in heavy, flocked wallpaper, stitching elaborate gowns for balls that...But no, she would have been too young for balls. And all of Mary's ideas about what life was like back then came from books, she realized. Scenes from *Little Women* and *Gone with the Wind* and *Little House on the Prairie* all converged in her mind to create an image that probably had very little basis in reality.

What had become of Frances Hartman? That was what she really wanted to know. This sampler captured Frances at a specific moment in time, a young girl just on the cusp of adult-hood. Had she grown up? Gotten married? Had a family? Had the stitching of this sampler prepared her for the life she would lead? Had she been happy? Had she grown up interested in spiders, or was that just a fleeting instance of rebellion? Mary tried to picture her, imagining a long brown braid and swishy hoop skirts. Or maybe red hair—yes, red, she thought. Long and beautiful. With freckles, undoubtedly.

"Mary?"

Mary's head snapped up. Martha was standing in front of her. Oh, dear. From the look on her face, it seemed likely she'd been there a while.

"Are you there?" Martha asked. Mary felt her cheeks flush. Martha had probably called her name more than once. This had happened before, of course. Sometimes Mary just got so caught up in daydreams that she tuned out the world around her.

"What has you so engrossed?" Martha leaned forward to take a look.

"I was just wondering about the girl who made this," Mary confessed.

Martha examined the piece. "Did that come in this morning?"

Mary nodded. "Nancy brought it in."

"It's nice. And that's a fair price. I bet it will sell quickly."

That was Martha. Focused on the practicalities. "Yes, I'm sure it will." Mary sighed and set the sampler aside. Then she looked up and saw that her sister had a strange look on her face. "What's wrong?"

"Probably nothing," Martha said.

"You wouldn't have that look on your face if it was nothing," Mary said.

Martha hesitated for a moment, and then she said, "There's a car parked by the side of the road."

"Where?"

"Out on the road that runs past the Stoltzfus farm."

"Safe to say it doesn't belong to them," Mary said. The Stoltzfus family was Amish, and the Amish didn't drive cars.

"It looked like it had been abandoned," Martha said. "I noticed it at first when I was on my way to the grocery store, and figured there was a logical explanation for it. But it was there when I came back, so I stopped and peeked in."

Mary waved as a pair of customers, a young couple she didn't recognize, stepped inside the barn, and then she gestured for Martha to continue.

"I know it's probably nothing, but after what happened last night, I wondered..."

"You wondered if the phone and the car could be connected," Mary said. "It's a good question."

"The engine was cold, so the car has been there a while. And there was no one around. So whatever happened there wasn't recent."

"Maybe someone had car trouble."

"That's what I thought too," Martha said. "Maybe that's all it is."

"You wouldn't be telling me this if you really believed that," Mary said. She knew her sister too well. Martha was troubled by what she'd seen.

"It was only about half a mile from where Elizabeth and John found that phone," Martha said. "And it's so rare to see a car abandoned like that. I just wondered..."

"There has to be a way to figure out if they're connected," Mary said.

"I was hoping I could figure out whose car it was. Then I could maybe find out if they're fine or if there's something strange going on. So I took a picture of the license plate. When I went inside to unload the groceries, I tried searching for the name of the owner using that. But apparently that's not public data."

"That's probably a good thing," Mary said. "Though it doesn't help us in this case." She watched as the young couple examined a vintage Remington typewriter in the first aisle. "Do you think we should ask John to take a look?"

"I hate to waste his time if this turns out to be nothing." Martha leaned against the counter.

"But if it turns out to be something, you'd regret not mentioning it," Mary said. "It sounds like you should give John a call. He should be able to figure out who the car belongs to pretty easily. That will give him a name that might turn out to be connected to the phone."

"Okay." Martha nodded. "You're right."

"But..."

"But what?"

"You're not telling me something." Her sister couldn't hide things from her if she tried.

Martha let out a long sigh. "It's not a big deal. But maybe it will help us figure out whose car it is. I saw a receipt from the store on the passenger seat."

"From *our* store?" Mary felt silly even as the words came out of her mouth. What other store would Martha be talking about?

"From last Saturday. A week ago."

Mary had figured out that last Saturday was a week ago, but she bit her tongue. "Did it say what the person bought?"

"The purchase was rung up as linens."

"Huh." Mary sat back on her stool. "It shouldn't be that hard to figure out who we sold linens to last Saturday. There can't be that many people."

"That's what I was hoping," Martha said.

"I was in the store most of the day," Mary said. "Let me think about it, and I'll try to remember. We can ask Elizabeth too." Elizabeth was finishing getting ready for the day and would be over to the shop shortly.

"I'll try to think back as well," Martha said. "For now, I'll head over to the house and call John."

"That sounds good."

As soon as Martha headed out of the store, several customers came in, and Mary spent the next half hour ringing up purchases—the young couple took the typewriter—and helping one lady sort through a bin of assorted flatware in hopes of finding a spoon in the Arbor Rose pattern. Mary had no earthly idea what Arbor Rose flatware looked like, but the woman eventually located one and left the store happy. Then there was a lull, and Mary spent some time thinking back to last Saturday. Hadn't Diane Presley come in that day? Mary had gone to high school with her, but they hadn't seen each other in ages, so they spent some time catching up. Mary was pretty sure that was Saturday, because Diane had been looking for a used sheet to use as a screen to project a movie on for her church's youth group Sunday night. Mary wrote Diane's name on a scrap of paper and thought some more, but she couldn't keep her mind from wandering. She kept glancing at the sampler still lying on the counter.

She couldn't help wondering who Frances Hartman was and what had become of her. It was silly, Mary knew. She was clearly long gone—she would be nearly a hundred and fifty now—and there probably wasn't any way to find out anything about her life. But still, she wondered.

It wasn't going to go away, Mary realized. She was curious, and now that her interest had been raised, the only way to satisfy it would be to see what, if anything, she could learn about Frances. What could it hurt to do a little research and see if she could find out something about her? She thought the public library had some genealogical records, and she could no doubt find some information online. Maybe she'd turn up nothing, but she might learn something. Maybe she'd learn that Frances had grown up to be an incredible artist—one whose work was somehow lost to the centuries. Maybe she was like Florence Nightingale, tending to the wounded on the battlefields of World War I. Maybe she'd find out Frances had married young and had a dozen children. You never knew what you might uncover when you looked at history, Mary thought. She'd give it a shot. It would be fun.

CHAPTER FOUR

As soon as Elizabeth stepped into Secondhand Blessings, she saw that Mary was lost in a daydream. Well, there was no harm in that, she supposed. There were a few customers browsing, but no one seemed to need immediate help. But Martha, who had walked in with Elizabeth, was already calling out, "Earth to Mary."

Mary snapped out of her trance and smiled. "Hi there."

"You were lost in your thoughts. Anything fun?" Elizabeth asked. Goodness, it was warm in here. She'd need to bump up the AC. She shook out her T-shirt to get some air underneath it.

"Just wondering how to find out about a girl who lived a hundred and fifty years ago," Mary said. "But anyway. What did you all find out?"

Elizabeth wasn't sure how to respond, but luckily Martha spoke up.

"We talked with John and reported the car," she said. "He's going to check it out and said that if it looked suspicious he could run the license plates through their system to find out who owns the car."

"John also said they tried some of the obvious and common passwords but haven't been able to get the phone unlocked," Elizabeth reported. Ah...The breeze from the oscillating fan felt nice. "But he did say a text message had popped up."

"And he was able to read it?" Mary asked. Elizabeth had wondered the same thing. She had a cell phone, but she didn't use it all that much, and she tried to remember how it worked.

"You can set it to pop up a text message even when the phone is locked," Martha said. "The text shows up right on the lock screen."

"The message was from someone named Viv," Elizabeth said. "And it said, 'Where are you? You okay?'"

"I wonder what that means," Mary said.

Elizabeth shook her head. None of the possibilities that had flooded her mind were good.

"Most likely, it means someone is missing the girl who owns the phone," Martha said. "She didn't show up where she was supposed to."

No one said anything for a moment as they all absorbed that.

"Was John able to respond or find out anything more about who this Viv is?" Mary asked.

"Unfortunately, he would have had to unlock the phone for that," Martha said. "You can read the message, but you can't respond."

"Well, it's something." Mary was trying to be positive, Elizabeth could see. But she wasn't sure how it got them any closer to finding the missing girl to know that she had a friend named Viv.

"I'm sure John will do everything he can to find out about this Viv," Elizabeth said. "In the meantime, Martha and I came up with a list of people we sold linens to last Saturday."

"That's good," Mary said. "The only person I can remember selling something like that to is Diane Presley."

"She bought that sheet, right? To use for a projector screen?" Elizabeth remembered that.

"I came up with Janet Pelz and Alma Yoder," Martha said. "Janet bought that double-wedding-ring quilt with the pink and green flowers."

Elizabeth remembered that too. It was a beautiful quilt, not antique, but carefully hand-stitched and done in pretty pink and green calicoes. Janet had mentioned buying it as a wedding present.

"And Alma bought that set of towels," Mary said.

The towels had been brand-new with tags still on them, gleaned by Nancy VanSlyke from an estate sale. The sisters had met Alma a few months ago through their friend Rachel Fischer, who lived on the next farm over. Alma had been thrilled to find the towels. But Elizabeth had to laugh at the idea of the Amish woman being connected to the pink sparkly cell phone. The Amish didn't use cell phones except for their work or in emergencies. They didn't even have landlines in their homes; most kept a landline phone in a shed at the end of the driveway, and even then used them rarely.

Martha said, "It's hard to believe that phone belongs to her. But if we're tracking down every lead..."

"We need to consider every possibility," Elizabeth agreed. "I remember selling a doily to a woman named Chrissy Henry who lives in Strasburg." Elizabeth didn't know her but had chatted with her when she rang up the sale and told her that she'd remember Chrissy's last name because it was their father's name. She wished she remembered more about her, but that was all she could come up with.

"That's four names. That's a good place to start," Martha said.

"So what do we do? Should we talk to these people and ask if they know anything about an abandoned car or a missing iPhone?" Mary asked.

"I think we can probably find a more tactful way to say that," Elizabeth said. "But that would at least give us some place to start."

Martha pursed her lips, and Elizabeth could see that she wanted to say something. "What is it?"

"I've been thinking about what might have happened, and I can't help playing devil's advocate here. We've been assuming the abandoned car and the abandoned phone are connected."

"You were the one who thought they were," Mary reminded her.

"I know," Martha said. "And I still think they may be related. But I'm trying to work through the logical possibilities."

"What do you mean?" Mary asked.

"Well, why would someone leave their car by the side of the road?" Martha asked.

"She must have had car trouble," Elizabeth said. She'd figured out that much. "And she was walking to get help. Home, or to the nearest house, maybe."

"To the nearest house to do what?" Martha asked.

"To use their..." Even as the words came out of her mouth, Elizabeth realized how ridiculous they sounded. Twenty-five years ago, you would walk to the nearest house to use the phone if you had car trouble. Now, you would just use your cell phone.

"Maybe she did call for help," Mary said. "We haven't seen her phone records. Maybe she had car trouble, and she called for help, and something happened to her as she walked toward help."

"Okay, let's say that's right," Martha said. "So our girl is walking along the road toward home, or the nearest house, and something happens. Let's go with your theory"—she glanced at Mary—"and this is like the Amber Barber disappearance. A car slows down, she realizes something isn't right. What does she do?"

"She sets her phone to blink SOS," Elizabeth said. And again, immediately felt foolish.

"Why wouldn't she, you know, use her phone to call for help?" Martha asked.

"Again, maybe she did," Mary said. "We haven't seen her phone records. Maybe she called for help, and then set her phone to blink SOS."

"John said the police hadn't received any calls for help." Elizabeth hated to remind them, because it put all kinds of holes in her theories. But they had to look at all angles if they wanted to find the truth.

"Maybe she didn't have time. Maybe it happened so quickly that all she had time for was setting her phone to blink SOS," Mary said.

"Do you see how unlikely that is?" Martha asked. "So few people even know the distress signal. Why would that be anyone's first response? Wouldn't her first thought be to dial 911?"

"Maybe it was all she could do." Elizabeth was getting frustrated. Why was Martha trying to knock down all their theories?

"Why leave the phone behind though?" Martha continued. "If she was getting kidnapped, why wouldn't she keep it with her? Then the police could use its GPS capabilities to track where she'd gone."

Elizabeth appreciated her sister's logical mind, though right now she was finding it maddening. "If she struggled with her kidnapper, it could have easily fallen out of her hands," Elizabeth said. It seemed so obvious. "He knew that she couldn't have her phone, or else the police would know where to find her."

"Maybe," Martha said.

Maybe? Why was she being so obtuse? That had to be how it had played out. "What other explanation could there be?"

"I don't know," Martha said. "I'm just asking questions. Maybe there's something we're missing."

Maybe there was. But Elizabeth couldn't see what it was, and with every second they were guessing, the girl was getting farther and farther from getting help.

"What are you all so serious about?"

Elizabeth recognized the inflection as much as the voice. She looked up and smiled at her friend Rachel Fischer, who was walking toward them.

"Hi, Rachel. We didn't see you come in."

"I know. You were all very absorbed in something," Rachel said with a smile. Rachel lived on a farm next to the Classens with her husband Silas and their eight children, and Elizabeth had gotten to know her pretty well through the years. She was kind and thoughtful, bringing food regularly when Mama's cancer advanced, and checking in during the long winter months to make sure Elizabeth and Mama were all right. She'd even sent her teenage boys Luke and Ephraim to shovel her driveway after a bad storm last February, a gesture so thoughtful it had brought tears to Elizabeth's eyes. "What is going on?"

Elizabeth glanced at her sisters. This wasn't a secret, was it? But Mary was already talking.

"Elizabeth and Officer John Marks found a phone by the side of the road last night." Mary explained the situation and their theory that the girl had been abducted. Rachel hadn't lived in the area when Amber Barber had disappeared—she'd moved here as a bride twenty-some years ago—and so they told her about how the girl had never been found and about their concerns that the kidnapper had struck again.

"Where was the phone found?" Rachel asked. Her brow was wrinkled, her eyes thoughtful. Her long brown hair was almost entirely covered by her white prayer *kapp*.

"Over on Harvest Drive, near where it meets Irishtown Road," Elizabeth said.

"What time was this?" Rachel asked.

"A little after eight thirty," Elizabeth said.

"That is interesting." Rachel was quiet for a moment, biting her lip.

"What do you mean, interesting?" Martha cocked her head.

Rachel didn't answer at first, and Elizabeth knew better than to rush her. Like most of the Amish that she knew, Rachel thought through what she was going to say before she said it.

Sometimes this led to pauses that felt awkward to Elizabeth but were a normal part of conversation for Rachel.

"I was speaking to Esther Detweiler this morning," Rachel said. "And she told me she had been talking with Roseanna Mast. The Masts were coming home from visiting the Lapp family last night."

Elizabeth was constantly impressed by the speed and accuracy of the Amish telephone, which was what they called the network that spread gossip and news throughout the community. Elizabeth had never been able to figure out how it worked, since they did not text or keep phones in their homes, but somehow news always spread quickly.

"You know Linda and Roseanna are sisters?" Rachel continued. "They are very close in age. Practically twins, and they still see each other as much as they can. Linda's first grandchild had just been born, and Roseanna wanted to meet the baby."

Elizabeth nodded, though truthfully she wasn't even sure who Rachel was talking about. So many of the Amish shared the same handful of last names that it was often difficult to keep track.

"Well, the Masts wanted to make it home before dark, but there had been some trouble with one of their horses." The Mast family was, of course, coming home in a buggy. "Abe does not like driving home in the dark, but he will not let Stephen do it, even though Stephen is perfectly capable. It drives Roseanna crazy. So Roseanna was on edge anyway, and she told me that Abe nearly blew up when a car zoomed past them. Abe has been very upset about speeding cars for a while now, especially after that bad accident a few years ago."

Accidents involving slow-moving buggies, which didn't have headlights and could be hard to see on dark roads, had been escalating in recent years, but the accident Rachel was referring to had been particularly grim. A speeding car had plowed into a buggy driving at night and had killed three people.

"Abe likes to report cars he sees speeding, so he was trying to see what kind of car it was, but Roseanna said the car then did something strange. It pulled over to the side of the road and stopped for a while."

"Really?" Elizabeth said at the same time that Martha said, "For how long?"

"I do not know how long it was pulled over, but Roseanna was hopeful it had stopped because the driver realized he had scared them and wanted to apologize."

Elizabeth could believe that. She remembered that Martha had just recently apologized to an Amish family for driving too quickly around their buggy.

"But the car drove away before Abe could read the license plate, and he was even more upset." Rachel pressed her lips together. "According to Roseanna, it zoomed away even faster than it was going when they saw it at first." A pause, and then she added, "I do not know if it is connected to what you saw, but it was in the same area at about the same time."

Elizabeth glanced at her sisters now. It sounded like they had an eyewitness to whatever had transpired out there on that country road last night. They might need to make a visit to Roseanna Mast to find out what she could tell them.

"That is very interesting," Martha said, smiling at Rachel. "Thank you for telling us."

"I think we'd like to talk to Roseanna, if that's possible," Mary said. "We're all very worried about what happened last night, and it sounds like she might be able to tell us what she saw."

"I am sure she would be happy to talk with you." The strings on Rachel's kapp bounced as she nodded.

"Where does she live?" Elizabeth asked.

"How about this?" Rachel smiled. "I need to run a few errands while I am in town, and then I need to get home and help Phoebe get ready to make her deliveries." Phoebe was Rachel's twenty-year-old daughter who had Down syndrome. She delivered milk and cheese to local families, including the Classen sisters, always with a big smile on her face. "But I will give Roseanna a call and see if she can talk to you this afternoon about what she saw last night. If she can, I will go with you to introduce you."

Elizabeth felt a sense of relief. "That would be wonderful." If Rachel came along, Roseanna would be much more likely to talk than if three random Englisch women simply showed up asking questions.

"All right then. I must go to the fabric store and the market, but I will give you a call after I talk with Roseanna."

"That's perfect," Martha said.

Rachel turned to go, but before she'd gone more than a few feet, she spun back around, her navy skirts flying. "I almost forgot why I came in here in the first place. I wanted to ask if it would be all right if the quilting circle started a half hour later this week. Miriam Troyer has her brother-in-law coming to stay, and she wanted to be home when he arrived."

"Yes, that should be fine," Elizabeth said, seeing that her sisters were nodding. Rachel's quilting circle had started meeting in the shop a couple of weeks ago on Thursday mornings to work on their quilts, but the store was otherwise generally very quiet at that time of day. It wouldn't matter if they started a bit later than usual.

"Thank you. I will be back soon."

As soon as she was gone, Martha said, "Well, that's an interesting development."

The sisters were silent for a moment, each lost in her own thoughts. And then, a few moments later, Mary quietly said, "Do you think the person who abducted Amber Barber is still around?"

"There's no way to know," Martha said. "And even if the answer is yes, there's no reason to assume this had anything to do with that."

Elizabeth wanted to believe her sister's words, but she still felt a shiver go through her. She said a prayer for the girl, whoever she was, but it didn't make her feel any better.

CHAPTER FIVE

Martha tried to keep herself focused on the tasks on her list—dusting the shelves, entering and pricing the new inventory, helping customers, ringing up sales—but her eyes kept darting over to the door. She knew she wouldn't miss them when they arrived, but still, she couldn't help glancing toward the driveway, just in case.

It was almost noon when she heard another car pull into the driveway, and she moved so she could see out the doorway. She could tell right away that this was a rental. It was too shiny, too new, and what state was that license plate from? She couldn't tell, but it wasn't the blue and gold of a Pennsylvania plate. She pulled off her apron and hurried toward the door.

And there they were. Dylan was spinning in a circle, arms outstretched, letting out energy after being cooped up while traveling. He was taller and leaner than the last time she'd seen him, and his hair was cropped short. And there was Craig, a tiny bit grayer, but still her sweet-tempered eldest. Her heart swelled looking at him. He'd turned out well, and he had a good, stable job and a beautiful family. And he looked more like Chuck with every passing year. Then Molly stepped out of the car in slim-fitting jeans and some kind of high-heeled sandal, her curly brown hair pulled back into a pony-tail. Molly was beautiful, and she loved Craig, and Martha was proud to call her a daughter-in-love. And then there was thirteen-year-old Kevin. He was...well, he was still sitting in the back seat of the car absorbed in something. Probably finishing up a game of some sort, Martha figured. He'd always loved video games.

"Grandma!" Dylan had stopped spinning and spotted her standing in the doorway. A second later, he was flinging himself at her, and she wrapped her arms around him and pulled him in close. He had lost that little-boy scent, and he was bony and muscled where he used to be soft and squishy, but he was still her sweet Dylan, and nothing felt better than having him in her arms at last.

"Hi, Mom," Craig said, walking around the front of the car. He came up behind Dylan, and as soon as his son let go, he leaned in to give her a hug.

"Hello, Craig. How was the trip?" She pulled him in tight, and he gave her a quick hug and then released her too quickly.

"Long," Craig said. "But we're glad to be here."

"Hello, Mom," Molly said, coming up beside her husband. Martha smiled and pulled her in for a hug. Molly was thin and pretty, and she'd always been pleasant, though she and Martha came from different worlds.

"Hi there. I'm so glad you're here."

"We're glad to be here." Molly adjusted her tortoiseshell sunglasses and stretched her arms over her head. "Now where's Dylan off to?"

"They have goats!" Dylan was shouting as he made a bee-line across the yard toward the goat pens. Martha laughed. Yes, they had pygmy goats. Craig and his family had been to the farm six months ago, for Mama's funeral, but the goats came after that. "Kevin, check it out! Goats!"

But Kevin was still sitting in the back seat, staring down at a screen. Molly shook her head and marched over to the far side of the car.

"Kevin, get out here now and say hello to your grand-mother," she said. Kevin's response was inaudible. A few moments later, he stepped out of the car and looked around, blinking in the bright sun.

"Hey, Grandma," he said. A moment later, he looked back down at his screen. A phone, she could see now.

"Go give her a hug," Molly said, taking the phone from his hands.

Kevin's response wasn't exactly a sigh, but it was something like it. He made his way toward Martha and leaned in for a hug, but didn't put his arms around her. Still, she pulled him in close, drinking in the feel of him. She'd known she'd miss her grandchildren when she moved here, that it would take a lot more effort to see them than it had when they all lived within driving distance, but she hadn't realized how much they would change since she saw them last. Kevin was bulkier, some-how, and had a sprinkling of acne on his cheeks and a few fine whiskers just barely visible on his chin. He'd start shaving soon, she supposed.

"It's so good to see you."

"You too," he said, and then pulled back and turned around. He held out his hand for his phone. Molly shook her head.

"Not until we get these bags into the house," she said.

Kevin sighed again. "I'm in the middle of a *conversation*."

"And now it's time to have a conversation with us." Molly slipped his phone into her pocket and pointed toward the back of the car. Kevin glared at her, but he moved toward the back of the car and slapped the trunk. Craig pushed a button on the key fob, and the trunk popped open.

A few minutes later, Martha had gotten Craig and Molly settled into the guest room and helped the boys set up air mattresses in the attic, and then the family gathered in the kitchen while she made them lunch. Well, Craig and Molly and Kevin did. Dylan had gone out to play with the goats again. Good for him, Martha thought. These kids were growing up disconnected from the natural rhythm of agrarian life, and it was good for him to experience it.

"Please let me help, Mom," Molly said for the third time.

"No, no. You rest." Martha gestured toward the table. Martha enjoyed cooking for them. "Tell me what's been going on with you all."

"We've been busy as usual," Molly said. That was the mantra of families these days, Martha thought. Busy. They almost wore it like a badge of pride. "Dylan's travel hockey team has started up practice already, and Kevin has been doing all kinds of day camps—coding and chess and, oh, I don't know. What else, Kev?"

But he didn't look up from his phone. Had he not heard, or was he ignoring his mother?

"Kevin," Craig said, in a tone that got his attention. "Your mother asked you a question."

Kevin's head snapped up. "What?"

"Tell Grandma about the camps you've been going to this summer."

Kevin sighed, like telling his grandma anything was the last thing he wanted to do.

"Oh. Yeah. Chess camp, computer camp, math camp." He shrugged. "They're cool." Then he looked back down at his phone.

"So you enjoy them?" Martha asked.

"Sure." He didn't even look up from his screen.

"The guidance counselor at the high school said it will give him an advantage once school starts, and it's good for his college resume," Molly said with a shrug.

Martha smiled, unsure what else to do, but inside, she was conflicted. Maybe it was good for them. But her kids had always spent the summers roaming the neighborhoods, playing in the woods at the edge of the developments, and driving the lifeguards nuts at the local pools, finding ways to entertain themselves. What happened to the long, lazy days of summer? Was that why Kevin wouldn't look up from his screen now? He was so taxed that he had to relax when he could?

"Kevin?"

He reluctantly looked up at the tone of his father's voice.

"What did we tell you about the phone?" Craig crossed his arms over his chest.

"I just need to finish this game. Ethan is waiting for me to—"

"*Now.*" Craig's tone brooked no argument.

Kevin muttered something Martha couldn't quite make out, but he slipped the phone into his pocket.

Well. That was overdue, but at least he'd listened.

"Now then. Would you like to go outside and see the animals?"

The look on Kevin's face said it all. He didn't want to do anything but sit here and look down at that little screen.

"I'd love to poke around inside that store. What a cute place," Molly said.

"Well then," Craig said. "Let's go check out Secondhand Blessings."

Kevin didn't argue, but he did touch his pocket as he stood, probably to make sure his phone was still there.

Martha tried not to let it bother her. He was thirteen. Of course he was more interested in what was on his phone than looking at antiques and farm animals. But if she was honest, it still stung.

CHAPTER SIX

It had been a busy morning in the shop, and with Martha occupied with her family's visit, Elizabeth had barely had a chance to breathe. Summer was prime tourist season in Lancaster County, and Elizabeth reminded herself to be grateful for these busy days, since hopefully they would sustain them through the leaner winter months. But still, she was so absorbed in ringing up sales that she didn't even notice John Marks until he appeared right in front of her.

"Oh. Hello." Elizabeth laughed and smoothed her hand through her hair. The humidity was probably making it look crazy right now.

"I didn't mean to surprise you."

"No, you didn't." Wait. "I mean, you did, but it's good to see you."

Mary had been straightening the kitchenwares, creating a display to feature the set of Fiestaware that had recently come in, but she set the dishes down and came over to hear what John had to say.

John laughed, and the little lines around his eyes crinkled. "I can see that you're busy here, so I won't keep you."

Elizabeth wanted to interrupt, to tell him that he wasn't interrupting, that she wanted to talk with him, but she didn't know how to say it without sounding crazy, so instead she said,

"Is there any news about the phone? Were you able to get it unlocked?"

"I'm afraid not. Not yet anyway. Our team is working on it, but the tricky part is that when you guess wrong, the phone becomes disabled for escalating periods of time."

He must have seen the confusion on their faces, because he continued. "After five wrong attempts, the phone locks up for a minute. After six, it locks up for five minutes. Then fifteen, and so on. The difficult thing is that there's a security feature that will completely erase all the data on the phone after ten failed attempts to log in. We don't know if the phone has this feature turned on or not, and we obviously don't want to erase the phone data, so we don't want to enter the wrong passcode too many times."

Elizabeth nodded, following. If the data on the phone was erased, they'd lose all the photos, texts, recent calls, recent GPS locations, contacts, and everything else that would hopefully allow them to figure out who the owner was and what had happened to her.

"And there's no way to tell if the security feature is turned on without getting into the phone," Elizabeth said.

"Bingo." John shrugged. "In some ways, we're lucky the phone is a few years old. The newest phones have face recognition software, and it's possible to set them so that the only way to unlock them is for the phone's owner to look directly at the screen."

"That's creepy," Mary said. "The phone can recognize your face?"

"The newer ones can," John confirmed. "And if this were one of those models, we would never be able to get it open."

"Is all this security necessary?" Mary asked. Elizabeth felt the same way. If someone got into her phone, all they'd find out was that she liked to play praise music and keep in touch with her friends from church.

"Sure. Even if you don't keep state secrets in your email, someone with bad intentions could find out phone numbers of your contacts and passwords and all sorts of information. Typing in a passcode is a pain, but it's important."

Elizabeth reluctantly agreed.

"And we don't have any information about the girl yet. We're hoping to work with the phone company to get access to phone records, but since we don't know the phone number, it's proving very difficult."

"Oh." She tried not to sound disappointed.

"But several more texts came through from that Viv person," John said. "She's gotten increasingly worried about where our girl is. It seems she was supposed to meet up with Viv, whoever she is, last night, but never did."

"Oh dear." Elizabeth didn't like the sound of that at all.

"And I do have some news about that car Martha spotted by the side of the road this morning."

"What did you find out?" Mary asked.

"I went to check it out for myself this morning," John said. "But when I got there, it was gone."

"Gone?" Elizabeth felt silly repeating the word, but it slipped out before she could stop herself.

"Unfortunately, yes. There were tire marks in the grass, so I could see where it had been, but the car was gone by the time I arrived."

Elizabeth looked at Mary. What did this mean?

"Now, it could mean nothing. Maybe it was just someone who had car trouble and got the car towed away. Maybe someone parked there for the night for reasons that make sense to them. It's hard to say."

"Yes, but..." Mary struggled for words, and Elizabeth could see the same confusion she felt on her sister's face. They had been so sure the car was connected to the missing girl.

"But I do agree that it seems likely there's a connection between the car and the phone we found last night," John continued, and Elizabeth saw her own relief mirrored on her sister's face. "I was able to run the plates using those photos Martha sent me," he said. "And it turns out the car is registered to a Jack DiNapoli, in State College."

"Jack DiNapoli?" Mary repeated the name.

Elizabeth shook her head. She didn't know anyone named Jack DiNapoli.

"We've tried to get in touch with him but haven't had any luck yet," John said. "But I did want to let you know we are working on it."

"We appreciate it," Elizabeth said. "And we have news too."

"What's that?" John asked.

"Rachel Fischer was in here a while ago. She said an Amish family reported seeing a car speeding on Harvest Drive last night, right near where we found the phone. Apparently the car pulled over to the side of the road and then zoomed away."

"When was this?"

"Rachel wasn't sure exactly, but it was after dark and in the same place. It's probably worth talking to them."

"Ah. Right." John nodded. "We did get a call from Abe Mast last night, reporting a car speeding."

Why did he look so unconcerned? Something wasn't right.

"Don't you think it could be connected to the missing girl?" Elizabeth asked.

"I guess we can't rule it out," John said. "But he calls to report speeding cars at least once a week. I didn't even know Amish people were allowed to use phones as often as he does. He's always trying to get us to come out and arrest people based on a license plate number he wrote down or something. Don't get me wrong—the speeding really is a problem. But unfortunately, it doesn't work like that. We can't just arrest or ticket people based on someone calling to report them."

"Of course not." Apparently the police were familiar with the Masts. "But isn't it worth finding out?"

"I'll talk to the guys at the station about it," John said. He tried to hide it, but his voice betrayed the lack of enthusiasm he had about this lead.

Someone cleared their throat, and Elizabeth looked up to see two customers waiting at the register.

"Oh goodness, we're so sorry." Mary rushed over to the register and started to ring up the purchases.

John laughed. "I should let you all get back to work. But I wanted to let you know what we'd found out."

After seeing John to the door, Elizabeth returned to the register. "Are you getting hungry?" she asked her sister, but Mary didn't seem to have heard her. She was staring down at that embroidered piece that had come in earlier. "Mary?"

"Oh, I'm sorry." Mary spun around. "Were you talking to me?"

"I wanted to see if you wanted to take your lunch break now. I came in later than you, so it's fair if you want to go first."

Mary looked out over the store. "Are you sure you can hold down the fort on your own?"

"Martha promised to come back when Rachel calls," Elizabeth said. "And there seems to be a bit of a lull now." There often was a slow period around this time, while people ate lunch. "It seems like a good time."

"All right," Mary said. She glanced back down at the embroidery. "Actually, maybe I'll use this time to visit a couple of the customers who bought linens, to see if they know anything about the missing girl."

"That would be great." They had four people to check in with, and if Mary was prepared to cross one item off their list on her lunch break, so much the better. "How about I stop in and see Diane Presley?" Mary said. "I'll also see if I can find an address for Janet Pelz."

"Sounds great."

"All right." Mary slipped her apron over her head and started toward the door. "I'll be back as soon as I can."

"No rush. I had a big breakfast."

Elizabeth surveyed the store as Mary stepped out into the bright day. There were a few customers browsing the racks of secondhand clothing, but otherwise the store was quiet. There were stacks of things to be inventoried and mounds of paperwork to deal with, and there was always dusting and cleaning to be done, but while there was a moment of peace, Elizabeth decided to do some investigating of her own.

She turned to the computer, moved the mouse to wake the screen up, and opened a browser window. She typed in the name Jack DiNapoli and hit RETURN.

Pages and pages of results came up. There was an actor by that name, and a businessman who ran a large technology company, and a writer. Were any of these the right person? She had no idea. Then, she ran the search again, adding the words *State College, PA*.

This time, her search returned a Twitter account. She clicked on it and found a photo of a young man with brown hair and a short beard wearing a blue and silver football jersey. It was hard to tell exactly, but judging by the brown foamy beverage in his hand, she guessed he was a fan at a tailgate and not a player. But she recognized the lion's head logo on the jersey as belonging to Penn State, which was in State College, Pennsylvania. He was likely a student at the enormous state school, then. She scanned his posts. Retweets of various jokes that she didn't find funny, some strident political views—why did people feel the need to post those online, she wondered—and a few pithy observations about current events. Nothing too surprising. And nothing that gave her any indication of why his car might have ended up at the side of the road this morning—or where it had gone after that.

Elizabeth continued to search, but she didn't find any contact information for him or anything that got her any closer to figuring out how—if?—Jack DiNapoli was tied up in all this.

Elizabeth looked around the shop again, trying to find a way that this all made sense, but nothing came to mind. But her eyes landed on the shelves of books, and she had an idea. Hadn't she seen...? She came around the counter and walked over to the rows of used books. She'd seen a book of naval history, she thought. She crouched down, and there it was, a thick cloth-bound volume on the bottom shelf. She had no idea where it had come from or who would want to buy it, but people often wanted things that surprised her. She pulled it off the shelf and opened the cover. She knew from John being in the navy that if she wanted to learn more about what SOS meant, this was a decent place to start. The book was printed on thick, heavy paper and was mostly text, but there were black-and-white photographs of ships throughout. It wasn't the kind of thing that would normally catch her eye, but Elizabeth flipped to the back and scanned the index.

There. SOS, page 263. Elizabeth turned to page 263 and read that SOS was a distress signal that ships would send out using Morse code before modern technology made communication much easier. It had started as a signal used by the Germans and had been adopted internationally. It was not, as she had assumed, an abbreviation for Save Our Ship, but a signal that was used because it was easily transmitted and recognizable with its three dots, followed by three dashes and three more dots.

Well, sure, it was simple enough to recognize if you knew Morse code, Elizabeth thought. Though she supposed most people on a ship would have known it, at least back in the day.

This didn't explain why the SOS signal was still used as a distress call today on a modern iPhone. Completely removed from any naval context, why were app developers still using the signal as a way to summon help when no one these days understood Morse code?

Then again, John had seen it and figured it out, she realized. True, he'd been in the navy, but so had many other people. Maybe it wasn't as ridiculous as it seemed at first. She closed the book and set it back on the shelf. Well, she'd learned something, but it wasn't getting her any closer to finding the missing girl.

And with every moment that passed, she couldn't help thinking time was running out.

CHAPTER SEVEN

Mary followed her GPS to the address she'd found for Janet Pelz. She'd found the address easily enough, and it was on the way to Diane Presley's home, so she figured she'd kill two birds with one stone. As she pulled into the driveway, she noticed that the Pelz home was a farmhouse surrounded by fields. A wooden barn, painted a deep green, stood in the distance. The first thing Mary noticed when she stepped out was the silence. Her own home—the one she shared with her sisters—was never as still as this. They only had a few farm animals, but combined with the customers coming and going from the shop, there was always noise of some kind. But this place was quiet, and nothing moved—no dogs came running to investigate the sounds of the car, and no one came out of the house to see who was here.

There were no cars in the driveway. There was a small garage attached to the house, but the door was closed. Even before she'd climbed up the porch steps, she knew that there was no one home. She rang the doorbell anyway and waited while it rang inside, and rang again. She'd found a phone number for Janet in the same phone book where she'd found the address, and she dialed it now, but she could hear it ring inside the house, and no one picked up. Finally, she turned away and went down the stairs.

She'd struck out here, but she entered the address she'd found for her old friend Diane Presley into her phone, and a few minutes later pulled up in front of a beautiful two-story Victorian painted a grayish blue and dripping with lacy, white gingerbread trim. A London plane tree arched overhead, its gnarled branches spreading shadows over the wide green lawn. When Diane Presley had come into Secondhand Blessings a week ago, Mary had recognized her immediately, though she hadn't seen her in at least two decades. She somehow looked the same as she had in high school. They had caught up, Mary explaining that she'd moved back home to help run the family business with her sisters, and Diane talking about living in Lancaster and doing accounting and bookkeeping from her home office. A quick look at the phone book had given Mary the address, and fifteen minutes after she left the store, she was walking up the bluestone path toward the front door.

It was a beautiful home, and well kept, Mary thought. Diane had always been neat and organized. She'd been the captain of the girls' tennis team and also the student body treasurer. Mary had secretly envied her in high school. She'd always felt a bit in the shadows of her two older sisters and had never felt totally comfortable expressing herself in high school. But Diane had been gregarious and friendly, and Mary had genuinely enjoyed catching up with her last weekend. Now, she hoped Diane would respond just as pleasantly to this surprise visit. She pressed the doorbell, took a deep breath, and waited.

The bell echoed inside, but there was no answer. That was strange. There was a car in the driveway, a late-model European sports car. She pressed the bell again.

Mary waited again, but there was still no answer. She was about to turn to go, but just then the door opened, and Diane stood there. She wore light brown pants with dirt at the knees and a floppy hat, holding gardening gloves in one hand.

"Mary!" Diane's face broke into a smile. "How lovely to see you. I'm sorry, I didn't hear the bell at first. I was out back. Come in, come in."

She ushered Mary inside the cool house, and Mary took in the scraped hardwood floors, the light-colored walls covered with tasteful, calming artwork, and the mostly antique furniture. Mary traced her hand along the wood of the turned newel post.

"This is lovely," she said as Diane led her down the hall, past a chef's kitchen, toward an open set of french doors.

"Oh, thank you." Diane waved her hand, dismissing the comment. "This place needed a lot of work when we bought it, but we've fixed it up slowly over the years." She led them out onto a wooden patio planted with pots of geraniums and marigolds and lush herbs. "I've been weeding." She grimaced and gestured toward a raised-bed garden that took up a large section of the yard. She must have dozens of kinds of vegetables in there, Mary thought. She could see beans and peppers and tomatoes just from here.

"That's quite a garden," Mary said. She'd hoped to get Mama's garden back in shape, but this summer had been so busy that she hadn't gotten around to it. Maybe by next year.

"It is a lot of work, but I find it relaxing," Diane said. "Have a seat."

She gestured toward a wrought-iron table and chairs in the shade of a yellow umbrella, and Mary gratefully settled into a chair. Diane disappeared back inside, and a moment later, she came out carrying a tray of lemonade in a frosty pitcher and glasses. A soft breeze blew through the trees that surrounded the wide green lawn, and it was comfortable and pleasant here.

"Now then." Diane poured glasses of lemonade and sat down across from Mary. "How are things going?"

Mary took this as her cue to explain why she'd come. "I really enjoyed catching up with you when you were in the shop last Saturday," she said. She took a sip of the lemonade and tried to figure out how to phrase this without coming across as crazy. "And I do hope you'll come back again. But I have something of a strange question."

Diane smiled. "I'm all ears."

"I seem to remember that you bought a white sheet."

"Yes, to use as a screen to project a movie for the youth group."

"How did that go?"

"It was a blast. The kids had a great time. How often do you get to watch a movie outside?"

Mary had to admit it sounded like great fun. "I'm glad. Well, you see, the reason I'm here is that"—she took another sip, stalling, trying to get the words to come out right—"is that we're trying to talk to the people who bought linens at our store last Saturday. Because one of them might have something to do with an abandoned car at the side of the road."

Diane's eyes narrowed, and she seemed confused. Oh dear. Mary was making a mess of this.

"You see, my sister Martha saw a car at the side of the road this morning, and there was a receipt from our shop in the front seat. It was for last Saturday, for linens."

"Okay," Diane said, nodding slowly. "And you're trying to figure out who the car belongs to?"

"No, we know who the car belongs to, but we don't know why there's a receipt from our store in it. We think it might be connected to a kidnapping."

Diane gasped. "A kidnapping?"

Oh dear. Why had she said it like that? "A potential kidnapping," Mary clarified. "We're not really sure."

"Is someone missing?" Diane asked cautiously.

"We're not really sure," Mary said again. She picked up the glass of lemonade to buy herself time. It was cold, and the feel of condensation on the outside of the glass gave her something to focus on other than the mess she was making of this. "I guess the truth is, we're worried something bad happened, and we think the car at the side of the road and the receipt inside might be connected. So we're trying to talk to everyone who bought linens last Saturday, just to make sure."

"To make sure I haven't been kidnapped?" Diane grinned.

Mary let out a laugh. "No, I guess...Well, I'm not really sure, to be honest. I guess just to see if you know anything. We're just trying to follow any lead."

"Well, I can tell you with certainty that my receipt is where it should be in my file cabinet, and I don't know anything about an abandoned car or missing person."

Mary believed her, and though she felt a bit silly, it was still nice to catch up. They chatted for a while about Diane's work with the youth group at her church and what Mary had been up to in Indianapolis for so many years, and then Mary thanked her for the lemonade and headed back to the car. Diane had been gracious and kind, just as she'd always been, but she hadn't had any of the answers Mary was looking for.

Well, maybe she would find some at her next stop, Mary thought, pulling away from the curb. About ten minutes later, she had driven through the quiet streets of Lancaster and pulled into the parking lot behind the public library. The red brick building had a beautiful federal-style edifice with fluted columns and a triangular pediment with the words LANCASTER FREE PUBLIC LIBRARY on it, but the back entrance, accessible from the parking lot, was less grand, with its white-framed windows and small out-door reading area. Mary stepped inside the cool, quiet building, and felt like she'd come home. She loved the wooden shelving piled with neatly organized volumes and the historic paintings of men in uniforms in gilt frames along the walls. She loved the unmistakable scent of paper and glue and must that every library shared. Mary had spent many afternoons inside this building, reading and daydreaming, when she was younger, and she knew the general layout of the books on the first and second floors pretty well. But she wasn't here to look for books today, and she wasn't sure where exactly to go.

"You look lost."

Mary turned to find a woman about her age standing next to her. She had long brown hair threaded with silver, and a kind, round face.

"I was wondering where I would go to find old newspaper articles," Mary said.

"How old are we talking?" The woman's face lit up in a wide smile.

"About forty years or so," Mary said, doing some quick math in her head.

"Fun." She held her hands together. "Are you looking for local newspapers, or those from around the world?"

"Local, I think," Mary said.

"In that case, come right with me." She gestured for Mary to follow her and led her past a bank of computers and up a flight of stairs to a small alcove with two computer terminals. Lettering above them read RESEARCH TERMINALS.

"These computers are connected to all kinds of databases that will help you find old newspaper articles," the librarian said. She showed her how to log on with the barcode from the back of her library card, and then she pointed out several databases Mary could check. "This one will search the archives of the newspapers from around the state of Pennsylvania," she said. "There's some fun stuff in here, including back issues of *The Budget*."

Mary recognized the name of the weekly Amish newspaper and had to laugh at the idea of seeing it online.

"And this one is a more global database. Many more papers, and probably more comprehensive, but much less fun, in my humble opinion."

"Wow. All of this from a computer terminal?" Mary shook her head. "Whatever happened to those old machines that you had to thread that film through?"

"Microfilm?" The woman laughed. "And then you had to stare at the grainy screen to try to make out what it said?"

"And everything was orange?" Mary laughed.

"I miss it dearly," the librarian said. "But I will admit that this is more efficient."

"I suppose you have to change with the times," Mary said.

"But not too much, hopefully." The woman held out her hand. "I'm Kathleen. Head librarian and lover of all things historic."

"Mary Classen Baxter." Mary shook Kathleen's hand. "Fan of history, uncertain about the use of computer databases."

Kathleen smiled and showed her how to search inside the database and highlighted a few of the other research tools available on the terminal, including a genealogy database. Mary thanked her, and Kathleen told her to just ask if she needed anything.

Mary opened up a search screen and typed in the name Amber Barber. The first result that came up was an article in the *Lancaster Intelligencer Journal* from 2010. The headline read, THE DISAPPEARANCE OF AMBER BARBER: THIRTY YEARS LATER AND STILL NO ANSWERS.

Mary clicked on the link. The story reflected on the disappearance that had rocked the countryside, and reflected on the fact that though there had been various suspects through the years, the police had never found anything conclusive. While interesting, this article didn't tell her anything she didn't already know. Mary clicked back to the main search screen and kept going back to mid-October, 1980. There. That looked like the first article, from October 16. The headline on the front page read TEEN GIRL REPORTED MISSING; BIKE FOUND ABANDONED NEARBY. She clicked on the link and found the image of the article from the paper the day the story ran.

Amber Barber was reported missing by her parents, Jean and Michael Barber, at 6:30 Wednesday night, after she failed to return home from a visit to a neighbor's house. Amber was last seen leaving the home of Merry and Emery Brencher, where she had been visiting the Brenchers' daughter Hannah. Amber set off on her bike around 4:30, the Brenchers said, and she was familiar with the route, having ridden it many times. When Amber didn't arrive home, both families went out to search, and the police were called in when they were unable to locate her.

The case took a dark turn when, around 8:30 p.m., Amber's bike was found in a cornfield several miles away. As of press time, there have been no other clues regarding the whereabouts of Amber Barber, and anyone with any information is urged to come forward.

The next day's paper had the story splashed across the front page: NO TRACE OF AMBER BARBER; PARENTS AND POLICE INCREASINGLY CONCERNED. There was a school picture of Amber next to the article, and with her wavy shoulder-length brown hair and wide brown eyes, she looked childlike and innocent. The article contained no new information, but there were quotes from unnamed sources suggesting the girl had probably run away, and quotes from Amber's parents, insisting she had saved her allowance to buy that bike and would never leave it behind willingly. They begged anyone with information about what happened to her to come forward.

By October 18, the articles covering the disappearance took up the entire front page. One article was devoted to neighbors and friends who gave stirring testimonies to Amber's sweet character, and another covered the candlelight vigil held at her high school the previous night. The main article reported on the only break in the case so far—an Amish farmer had reported having seen a car racing away from the area at about 4:45 on Wednesday afternoon. The Amish farmer was unidentified, saying he wished to remain anonymous, but the police apparently believed his story was credible and were now on the lookout for a brown Toyota Celica with Pennsylvania plates. The newspaper printed a photo of a Celica, a hatchback that looked impossibly boxy by today's standards, as reference. After that fact was reported, talk of Amber being a runaway had disappeared, and police had focused on the case as a kidnapping. But it hadn't helped. The story stayed in the paper for weeks, but, as Mary and her sisters had remembered, no trace of Amber was ever found, and the story finally fell out of the papers aside from remembrances at various anniversaries.

Mary leaned back, and the old wooden chair creaked beneath her. She wasn't sure what she had been hoping to find, but she couldn't see anything in these old articles that was any help in determining whether or not this disappearance was related to Amber's. Sure, there were similarities—the phone had been abandoned in the same way that Amber's bike had been, for one, and it had been an Amish farmer in both cases that had seen a car driving away. But how could those facts have anything to do with...well, anything? Amber's disappearance had been almost forty years ago. Would the kidnapper even still be alive? She supposed it was possible, if he had been relatively young when Amber was taken. He could have struck again. But why, after all this time?

Mary looked through all the articles that mentioned Amber, but she didn't end up any closer to figuring out if the two incidents were related. She closed the search window and started to push herself back, but then her eye caught on a link to another database Kathleen had pointed out. Genealogy. She knew some people back in Indianapolis who had been heavily into genealogy, but Mary had never spent much time on it. Mama had her family Bible, which traced their family back four or five generations, and she'd known her great-grandparents on her father's side, Hester and Aaron Classen. Their people were Mennonites who had come over from Switzerland and Germany to live in a place where they were free to worship as they saw fit, and their spiritual heritage had been passed down through the generations of Classens.

She clicked on the link, and a window opened up. The page was a section of the website for Lancaster County, and was filled with links to dozens of databases. Mary squinted at the links to the left side of the page, scanning names like *Dental Diplomas Index 1881–1927*, *Orphans Court Minutes Index 1753–1829*, and *Widow Appraisements 1872–1920*. Mary found one labeled *Birth Records 1870–1906*, and she clicked on it. A file downloaded from the site, and she opened it. It was a list of names, organized alphabetically, from *Abel, Charles Abram* to *Zimmer, William Arthur*. Each name had a book number and file number next to it. Mary assumed these referenced some hard copy records somewhere. She scanned the list and found *Hartman, Frances Louisa*. Her records were in book 13, file 654.

Well. Mary had no idea what to do with this information, but she supposed if she was interested enough, she could track down Frances's original birth records in some file in the Lancaster County Archives.

But maybe there was more she could find in these files. She clicked on the link for marriage records from 1850–1895, and was pleased to find that, with a little searching, she pulled up a record for Frances Hartman and a Clarence Matthews in 1891. Frances would have been just twenty then. Mary's fingers hovered over the keys. Had she had children? Where had she lived? What had she done? When had she died? Mary didn't know if Frances and Clarence had stayed in the area or had moved out of the county. But she supposed there was really only one way to figure it out.

Mary clicked on the link for death records from 1884–1906, and she was surprised to see a scan of a handwritten ledger appear on the screen. She squinted, trying to make out the old-fashioned handwriting. *Anderson, Horace,* was written on the first line, and next to that, she read that he was thirty-six, single, and a laborer. His date of death was recorded as June 16, 1893. It was a handwritten record of all the deaths in the area, she realized, no doubt kept by a county clerk. Mary squinted at the screen as she scrolled down the pages, looking for any mention of Frances or Clarence. She got to the last page, unsure if she was relieved or not that they hadn't been listed. She then clicked the link for death records from 1894–1930, and this led to a long list of records. She scrolled through pages, squinting at the screen, and finally came across a record for Clarence Matthews, who had passed away in 1910. He was married, the record said, and had been forty-one at the time of his death. Mary felt a wave of sadness for Frances, left a widow at thirty-nine. What had she done once her husband was gone? How had she gone on? Mary continued to scroll through the records, but didn't see any death record for Frances. She wasn't sure where else to look, and she'd already been here far too long. Her sisters were probably getting impatient for her to get back to the shop.

"How's it going in here?"

Mary turned and saw Kathleen coming toward her. "It's going all right."

"Those don't look like newspaper articles." Kathleen came up behind Mary and looked at the screen. "Oh, wow. You found the historical records indexes. Now you're getting into the good stuff."

"I'm not sure I'm really finding much of anything," Mary said with a sigh.

"What exactly are you looking for?"

Mary hesitated. Could she really explain what she'd been looking for to Kathleen? Mary wasn't even sure she understood it herself. Would Kathleen think she was crazy?

"This is kind of strange," Mary said. "But the shop just received a beautiful cross-stitched sampler, and I was kind of interested in finding out what happened to the girl who made it."

"Ooh." Kathleen's eyes lit up. "Can I see?"

Mary pulled up the picture of the sampler on her phone and explained what she'd already discovered about Frances's life.

"The needlework really is exquisite," Kathleen said. "It's really unusual." She smiled. "Would it be all right with you if I did some digging to see what I can find out about Frances?"

"Are you serious?" Mary asked. "You would do that?"

"I would be happy to," Kathleen said. "I love this sort of historical research."

"It's probably a waste of your time," Mary said. "I don't have any real reason besides curiosity to figure out what happened to her."

"Curiosity about the past is enough of a motivation for me." Kathleen adjusted her glasses. "There are so many lessons we can glean for today by looking at the past."

"I couldn't agree more. But that doesn't mean you have time to go off on a wild-goose chase simply to satisfy my curiosity."

"I would enjoy trying to find answers for you," Kathleen said so earnestly that Mary had to believe she meant it.

"Thank you," Mary said. Kathleen took Mary's phone number and promised to keep her informed of what she learned, and then Mary headed back out to her car.

They may not be getting any closer to finding out what had happened to the girl by the side of the road the night before, but she felt like she was getting a tiny bit closer to finding answers to another of her questions.

CHAPTER EIGHT

Elizabeth sat at the kitchen table and flipped through the home design magazines Mary had bought while she was in town. Mary's trip to visit Diane had stretched out longer than either of them had anticipated, and it was nearly midafternoon by the time Elizabeth was tucking into the ham and cheese sandwich, but Mary's apology had been bolstered by her gift of glossy magazines. At first Elizabeth had been skeptical, but as she sat here now, flipping through the pages, she began to see the possibilities. One magazine featured very modern designs, with lots of clean lines and dark gray paint. There were even articles about immaculately designed tiny houses, no bigger than a closet. Elizabeth didn't understand that craze, but she had to admit that the ones featured on these pages were cleverly done, with beds that turned into tables and storage in the strangest places. Still, she needed room to stretch out. But as she looked through the pages, she started to see some of the appeal of the very modern interiors. The furniture was simple, with clean lines and minimal decoration. The rooms were mostly done in simple color schemes, and the aesthetic was rather minimalist. In reality, it wasn't too much different from Elizabeth's taste, though it looked very different on the surface. Could she see herself with a platform bed and crisp white bedding and a striking pendant lamp over a faux-fur rug? She tried to picture it in her room and had to admit it wasn't as terrible as she would have thought.

She set that magazine aside and opened the next one, which mostly featured historic homes that had been renovated in modern styles. There were sleek kitchen cabinets painted in deep blues and stainless steel subzero fridges and waterfall quartz counters mixed with traditional elements like subway tile backsplashes and tin ceilings. She liked the way they looked. Mixing original details with a more modern twist was strangely enticing. She set her sandwich down and looked around the kitchen. The old wooden cabinets were solidly built, but now that she was looking, they did show their age, even with the coat of white paint she'd given them. And the old butcher-block counters were scarred and dented and stained. She'd always thought of the marks on them as charming, evidence of decades of lovingly prepared meals, but now she saw that they just looked tired. How much better would it look with a dark granite, or a traditional marble? Maybe they could give the cabinets another coat of paint? Perhaps a warm gray this time?

Elizabeth imagined it for a moment, but then she shook her head and set that magazine aside. They weren't redoing the kitchen, at least not anytime soon. She needed to focus on her bedroom for now. She did like the way the bedrooms in this magazine mixed original antique details with modern touches, such as elaborately scrolled woodwork paired with beautiful cement tiles and antique iron bedsteads topped with bedding in modern designs. She didn't even mind the way that fireplace mantel looked painted in black, she realized.

Elizabeth set that magazine aside. She really should get back to the shop and help Mary, since Martha was out showing her grandkids around town. But she had time for just one more, she thought, and reached for another magazine. This one featured rooms done in a country look, with lots of baskets and gingham prints and quilted wall-hangings and crockery. It was nice, but why were there so many knickknacks? And why were there so many chickens everywhere? She did live in the country, so maybe this was—

A ringing sound made her jump. What in the...But then she realized it was her cell phone. She pushed the magazines aside and got up to find her purse, and she finally dug her phone out. It was John calling.

"Hi, John." She was out of breath, but it was only because of the frantic search for her phone.

"Hi there, Elizabeth. There's been an interesting development, and I thought Martha might be interested to hear about it. I didn't have her number."

"Oh?" She tried to ignore the feeling of disappointment that rushed through her. He wanted to talk to Martha. "What happened?"

"Another text came through on the cell phone we found last night."

"What did it say?"

"It said, 'You're not missing anything,'" John said.

"'You're not missing anything'? What does that mean?"

"I don't know." John's voice was calm, and it didn't betray anything. "But here's the interesting part. The text was from Jack DiNapoli."

"Really?" Elizabeth recognized the name of the man the car at the side of the road was registered to. She thought for a moment.

"So that car and the phone we found must be connected." Jack's name was programmed into the phone they'd found. Whoever owned the phone must know him. And the text message he'd sent was very vague, but Jack must know the girl well enough that she would have understood what he was saying.

"It's not a guarantee, but I think it's pretty likely," John said. "We are going to treat them as if they are related."

"Wow." Elizabeth processed this. No wonder he'd wanted to tell Martha. "That's a big development."

"At least it's a positive connection between the abandoned car and the abandoned phone. It means we'll focus on trying to track down Jack DiNapoli."

"That's great." And then she added, "I'll tell Martha. She'll be glad her hunch was right."

"Thank you," John said.

He ended the call, and she sat still, holding her phone in her hand. It probably made sense for the police to focus on Jack, she thought, and she and her sisters could focus on talking to the people who had bought linens. Mary had said Diane didn't seem to know anything about the car, but they still had three people to talk to. One of them *had* to have a connection to the abandoned car, and therefore the missing girl.

Martha's heart felt full. She was squished into the middle of the back seat of Craig's rental car between two adolescent boys, and she couldn't be happier about it. They'd gone into town to tour the quaint downtown of Bird-in-Hand, and Martha had enjoyed showing off the pretty little town. They'd gone into the Old Amish Store, after a stern warning from Molly to her children not to laugh at the way the Amish storekeepers dressed or talked, and then into a tiny store that sold Amish-made cheese and jam. They'd gone past the long-standing landmark Bird-in-Hand Family Restaurant and Smorgasbord, and poked around in the farmer's market, and stopped in at Greta's for some coffee. The bulletin board by the door was hung with ads for the upcoming county fair and handwritten ads for rooms listed for rent, used cars, and farm equipment. They'd ducked into the Log Cabin Quilt shop and poked around in Bookberries, where Molly had bought a recent thriller, set right there in Amish country. Finally, after a stop for homemade, hand-churned ice cream at Bird-in-Hand Bakery, they were headed back to the farm so Molly and Craig could rest and Martha could get back to helping her sisters in the store.

"What did you like best?" Molly asked from the front seat, licking a black-raspberry-and-chocolate-chunk ice-cream cone.

"The ice-cream place," Dylan said. He had already finished his two scoops of chocolate/peanut butter swirl and had a streak of chocolate on his cheek that Martha didn't have the heart to point out.

"I should have guessed that one," Molly said. "How about you, Kevin?"

Kevin didn't answer. He was staring down at his phone.

"Kevin?" Molly asked again.

He still didn't look up.

"Hey." Martha elbowed him gently. "Your mother is talking to you."

"Huh?" He looked up and glanced toward the front seat.

"What did you like best about the town?" Molly repeated.

"Um, I guess the bookstore." And then he looked right back down at the screen. Kevin had found a book he'd wanted—some kind of illustrated thing that Craig referred to as manga—and begged his parents to buy it for him, but he hadn't even looked at it since then and had spent just about every moment engrossed in something on his phone.

"Hey." Martha elbowed him again. "What's so interesting?"

"I'm talking to my friends."

Martha took a deep breath. She had been thirteen once too. Hadn't she thought her friends were the most important thing in the world? It was just that technology now allowed kids to be connected to each other 24/7.

"What are you talking about?"

"Fortnite." His eyes didn't leave the screen.

"What is that?"

"It's a dumb video game." Dylan was bouncing up and down in his seat. The sugar from the ice cream had wound him up, Martha could see.

"It's only the *best* video game." Kevin finally looked up long enough to roll his eyes at his brother, and then he looked down again.

She tried not to let it bother her. He was a teenager now. Of course he was more interested in his friends than anything else. But it still rankled. They had come all this way to visit, and now he was more interested in the people on his screen than the people who wanted to spend time with him in real life.

Martha thought for a moment, trying to decide whether to say something. What could she say though? *Hey, put your phone down and pay attention to the people who love you?* She had a feeling that wouldn't be well received. Instead, she swallowed her frustration and turned to Dylan.

"So you're not into Fortnite?"

"Nah. I'm into cars."

Martha had known this; Dylan had been obsessed with vehicles from the time he was a toddler. She'd bought more toy trucks for Christmas and birthdays than she could count. He pored over books and magazines about the car industry and watched races on television just about every weekend. And if being interested in cars meant he wasn't spending all his time staring at a screen, she was even more grateful.

"What is your favorite kind of car these days?"

Dylan launched into a discussion of the relative merits of some kind of Ferrari versus a model of Alfa Romeo. Martha wasn't sure she'd ever seen either kind of car in the real world—this was more pickup truck or horse-and-buggy country—but she enjoyed hearing Dylan's enthusiasm as he talked about what he loved. But as he chattered away, she heard the telltale ding that meant she had a message on her phone. She quietly reached into her purse and found the phone, then read the message on the screen.

JOHN CALLED TO SAY THE PHONE WE FOUND GOT A TEXT FROM JACK DINAPOLI. THE CAR YOU SAW IS DEFINITELY CONNECTED TO THE GIRL WHO LOST HER PHONE.

Well, that was interesting. She had had a feeling the abandoned car had been connected to the girl who'd lost her phone, but now there was proof.

"Grandma, *what's so interesting?*" Dylan said, his eyebrows raised.

Guilty. Martha put her phone into her pocket right away. "Sorry about that. Continue, please."

Dylan chattered on about cars, and she tried to listen, but her mind was focused on what Elizabeth had told her. What did it mean? How was the girl connected to the car—and how would it help them figure out who she was and what had happened to her?

They were going to be passing the spot where Elizabeth and John had found the phone in about half a mile, she realized. Hadn't John said something about tire marks? An idea popped into her head. Hadn't she seen this on a television show? There was some kind of database that allowed detectives to take a picture of the tread and figure out what kind of car left the marks behind.

"Craig, could you pull over just up ahead?"

"Sure. Are you okay?"

"Yes, I'm fine. I just want to check something out."

"Okay." He glanced back at her in the rearview mirror. She knew she should be grateful her son was concerned about her, but he needn't have worried. She may not be a spring chicken, but she was hardly infirm.

"Just up here, please." Elizabeth had said it was just before the bridge over the creek. Martha directed him to the approximate spot, and then, when he'd pulled to the side of the road, she turned to Dylan.

"I was hoping you could help me."

"How?" Dylan's eyebrows were scrunched up, and his head was cocked.

"Do you know anything about tires?"

"Sure."

Of course he did. She didn't know whether that would translate into being able to identify tire treads, or if they would even be visible, but it was worth a shot.

Martha gestured for him to open the car door, and when he climbed out, she followed a step behind. "We'll be right back," she called to Craig and Molly.

Ugh. The day's heat felt especially brutal after the air-conditioned car.

"What's going on?" Dylan asked. The light sprinkling of freckles on his nose faded in the bright sun.

"There should be tire tracks..." Martha scanned the soft ground at the side of the road and spotted them, about ten yards ahead of them. "Aha. Up there."

"Cool." Dylan skipped as he hurried toward them.

Martha looked down at the impressions in the mud, which showed the car that had left them behind had veered off to the shoulder on the right side of the road and then pulled back onto the road ten or fifteen feet beyond. The impressions were deepest—probably an inch deep at their max—at the farthest point off the road.

"I know it's a long shot, but I was hoping you might be able to tell me something about the car that left these tracks behind," Martha said, coming up next to him.

Dylan bent down and looked carefully at the tire tracks left in the mud.

"It was a truck or an SUV." He reached out his hand and pointed to the tracks. "See how deep these treads are?"

Martha nodded, though she didn't truthfully have any clue how to tell how deep the treads were relative to other treads.

"A car would have smaller treads. And they were all-terrain tires, not snow or weather tires, but that makes sense this time of year."

Martha looked at her grandson. His hair was sticking up in the back, and he wore a T-shirt that had a Pokemon character on it. She'd thought professionals might be able to figure all this out, but Dylan was just ten.

"That's amazing."

"And it looks like the suspension is worn out."

"How can you tell that?"

"See how the tread is a little less distinct in those diagonal patterns?"

She bent down and squinted, finally saw what he had noticed. The tread was a little less distinct in a few diagonal stripes. But she would never have noticed that on her own, and she certainly wouldn't have known what it meant.

"Where did you learn all this?"

He shrugged. "Online." And then he added, "I like cars."

He might like cars, but he'd also just demonstrated an extraordinary gift of deduction and observation. Maybe he'd be a detective someday. For now, though, the others were waiting, and...yep, Kevin was back to staring at his phone again.

"Thanks for your help," she said.

"I don't mind." With that, he took off running back toward the car, making some strange kind of shouting noise as he went. Martha had to laugh. He may show skills reminiscent of a real detective, but he was still a boy.

"Did you find out anything useful?" Molly asked as Martha scooted back into the car. Martha had filled them in on the missing phone and the abandoned car earlier, so Molly and Craig had no doubt guessed that this was related to that.

"Yes, as it turns out, your son knows a lot about tires," Martha said as she moved into the middle seat again.

Craig laughed. "Anything related to cars. And robots, and computers, and *Star Trek*, and—"

"Just about anything he gets interested in," Molly added.

Martha turned toward Dylan to see if the discussion was making him uncomfortable, but he was smiling.

"Well, I certainly appreciate your help," Martha said. So she was looking for a truck or an SUV with a worn-out suspension. Maybe a farm vehicle. Hopefully they would be able to talk to Abe Mast soon to find out more. "And if I need to know anything about robots or *Star Trek*, I know who to ask."

Dylan gave her a goofy smile, and then he turned and looked out the window as Craig pulled back onto the road.

"And if I need to know about what happens when your face is glued to your phone, I'll ask Kevin." Martha meant for it to sound jokey, but it came out a little more whiney than she'd intended.

Craig and Molly laughed, but Kevin didn't even look up.

CHAPTER NINE

Martha came back into the shop just as Elizabeth was ringing up the sale of a collection of toy figurines from the nineties. When the figurines came in last week, Elizabeth had been certain they'd be stuck with them forever, but Mary had insisted collectors valued items like these, even if they weren't still in the original packaging.

"How is it going in here?" Martha asked, approaching the counter.

"It turns out people will pay good money for Mighty Morphin Power Rangers figurines," Elizabeth said, shaking her head. "And he seemed to think ten dollars each was a steal."

"I will never understand humanity."

The serious tone in her voice made Elizabeth laugh, though she personally agreed. "We got rid of the Teenage Mutant Ninja Turtles figures too."

"I wonder who comes up with toy ideas," Martha said. "Do you think people just sit around a conference room table trying to think of the most ridiculous idea they can, and then they go ahead and make that toy?"

"I want that job," Elizabeth said. "Anyway, it's been busy. Mary is in the back sorting out a new load of donations we got, but it's been pretty steady up here."

"That's good news."

"How was your time with Craig and Molly and the kids?"

Martha hesitated just a touch too long before answering. "It was good. Really fun. They're back at the house resting now."

"But what?"

"Nothing. It's fine. We had a good time."

Something was bothering Martha, Elizabeth could see that plain as day, but she could also see that her sister didn't want to go into it right now.

"And guess what Dylan helped me figure out."

Martha told Elizabeth about the tire marks and that they were looking for a truck or an SUV.

"He should work for the police," Elizabeth said.

"Maybe someday he will."

"We should let John know." Elizabeth knew that the police were looking into the phone and had resources that she and her sisters didn't have, and it was possible they'd already figured out the type of car that had stopped near the girl with the phone, but it couldn't hurt to share what they had learned.

"Yes, we probably should."

"And we need to talk to the other people who bought linens in the shop last Saturday," Elizabeth said. She'd wanted Martha to enjoy the time with her family, but if she was honest, part of her had been anxiously waiting for Martha to get back. "Mary talked to Diane, and she didn't know Jack DiNapoli or anything about the car, but we still need to talk to the others."

Martha nodded as she slipped behind the counter.

"Do you want to go?" Martha asked. "You've been stuck here all day."

"I haven't been *stuck*." Elizabeth did enjoy working at the shop, and she'd had a break at lunch. "But I will admit that I haven't really stopped thinking about that missing girl. It would be nice to do something productive." She had found an address for Chrissy Henry in Strasburg during a lull in customers earlier. Alma Yoder wasn't listed in the phone book, but hopefully Rachel would be able to help with that. She could try and talk to Chrissy while they were waiting for Rachel to call.

"Then you should go."

"You really don't mind?"

"I don't. Please go find some answers for us."

Elizabeth popped into the back to tell Mary she was heading out and found her absorbed in a large hardcover book about life in Lancaster County in the nineteenth century. Mary explained that she had found the book in the batch of new donations and gotten a bit distracted but had been genuinely working on pricing before she'd become absorbed. Elizabeth was used to her sister's quirks and couldn't do much besides smile.

She climbed into the car, set her GPS to the address she'd found for Chrissy Henry, and pulled out of the driveway. The cool air from the vents felt heavenly. As she drove, she thought about the GPS function on her phone. How did her phone know exactly where she was? Didn't it have something to do with satellites or cell phone towers? She was sure she could look it up. But what interested her wasn't that exactly. Mary had mentioned that you could find your phone if you lost it by looking for it from another device.

Elizabeth wasn't sure how it worked exactly, but she now remembered she'd seen Mary do it earlier this year when she'd lost her cell phone. She'd logged into her computer, and it told her her phone was in the backyard. She'd found it on the fence of the goat pen, where she'd left it when she'd gotten distracted while feeding the animals.

She slipped her headset on and touched the screen to dial John's number.

"Hi, Elizabeth."

"Hi, John." She wasn't just making an excuse to call him; she had a genuine question. Besides, she needed to pass along what Dylan had discovered. "Any luck getting the phone unlocked?"

"None so far. And there still haven't been any reports of a missing girl."

"Then maybe she's not missing. Maybe there's something else going on."

"It's possible." But the tone in his voice made it clear he thought that was unlikely.

"I had an idea."

"What's that?"

"Is there any way to tell if she's used some kind of computer program to figure out where her phone is?"

"Good thinking. We did look into that, and the answer is no. Not while the phone is locked. Even if we had it unlocked, it would be difficult to see if someone was logging in through the cloud to find its location, but until we get it open, there's no way."

"Oh." They'd already thought of it, then. Elizabeth felt silly.

"It was a very good idea," John said brightly. "Thank you for suggesting it. We're still locked out of the phone, but we should be able to try again in another hour or so."

"Were you able to talk to Abe Mast?" Elizabeth asked.

"I'm trying to get a team to head over there later today," John said.

Elizabeth bit her lip. They didn't seem to be taking that lead very seriously. She supposed that if Abe called to report speeding cars regularly, she could see why. But wasn't it at least worth looking into? It may be a waste of time, but she still hoped to talk to Abe and Roseanna about what they'd seen.

"Oh, and Martha's grandson looked at the tire tracks left in the mud by where we found the phone, and he thinks it was an SUV or a truck that stopped there."

John laughed. "Martha's grandson figured that out?"

"Yes. Is he right?"

"Our forensics team is looking into it. But they have yet to issue any conclusions." He laughed again. "How old is this kid?"

"He's ten. And he says the truck has a wonky suspension, apparently."

"I'm going to see about getting this kid a job."

"I think he needs to finish grade school first."

"An intern then."

"I'll see what I can do," Elizabeth said. "I'll keep trying to find out more."

"And we'll do the same."

Just after she hung up, her phone rang, and the words Fischer Farm flashed up on her screen. Rachel was calling from the phone shed at the end of her driveway. Elizabeth answered the call.

"Hi, Rachel."

"Hello, Elizabeth. I hope I am not disturbing you."

"Not at all." Quite the opposite, in fact, if she was calling with information about the Amish farmer who'd seen the car. "What's going on?"

"I spoke with Roseanna Mast. It was her family that saw the car?"

"Yes. What did she say?"

"She said we should come speak to her husband about it."

"Okay. When is a good time?"

"Now would be good."

"Really?" Usually at this time, Rachel would be working on cooking dinner or weeding the garden or hanging up the wash or any one of a thousand chores that had to be done. Then again, at this time, Elizabeth was usually in the shop, so the timing really couldn't have been better.

"Really. Hannah is trying out a new recipe for pork rolls, so I do not have to worry about dinner." Hannah was Rachel's thirteen-year-old daughter.

Elizabeth was always impressed to hear how skilled Amish girls became in the kitchen at such young ages.

"And it is such a beautiful day, ain't so?" Rachel continued. "Why should we not take advantage of it?"

It was a gorgeous sunny day, the sky a striking shade of cerulean blue. But it was hot, and the Amish didn't have air conditioning. Elizabeth didn't know how they could stand it.

"That sounds great to me. I'm not far away. I'll come pick you up in a few."

It didn't take long for her to circle back and pull into the driveway of the farm next to their own. As she bumped along the rutted dirt, a boy in suspenders ran out from the barn toward the house, a beautiful golden retriever dog following just behind him. That would be one of Rachel's eight-year-old twins, but Elizabeth couldn't guess which one at this distance.

Elizabeth climbed out of the car and walked toward the large house, which was painted a clean, simple white. She walked up the wooden porch steps, but before she got to the door, Rachel came out, her long black skirt swirling around her.

"Hello." Elizabeth smiled to see her friend. The Classens had always been friendly with the Fischer family, but in the past few years, especially when Mama and Daddy had been ailing, she'd come to know Rachel much better and had found comfort and grace in their friendship. "Are you ready?"

"Of course."

They climbed into Elizabeth's car, and Rachel immediately cranked up the air conditioning and pointed the closest vent toward herself.

"Now I see why you were so excited to come with me," Elizabeth joked as she turned around and headed back down the driveway.

Rachel laughed. "It does feel good. I must speak to the bishop about allowing air conditioners in our homes. It would make more people want to remain Amish, yes?" Rachel gave her a crooked smile, and Elizabeth knew she was joking.

"So. Which way?"

"To the left," Rachel said. "The Masts live just beyond Weavertown Road. They own that furniture shop."

"Oh, I know where that is." Elizabeth checked both ways and pulled out. Many of the Amish in the area ran businesses from their homes or barns, and Elizabeth had been into Masts' Furniture, which was run out of a workshop and show-room on their property, a few times. They sold handcrafted wooden furniture and did repairs as well, though Elizabeth couldn't imagine there would be much to repair in the pieces they made themselves. She had been impressed by the crafts-manship and quality when she'd been in the shop.

While they drove, Rachel told her how Silas's mother, who lived in a *dawdy haus* behind the main house, had forgotten to turn off her stove and nearly burned down the home a few nights ago. Elizabeth knew Anke had memory problems and had always been impressed by how tirelessly Rachel cared for her.

"She is getting worse," Rachel said. "I do not know how much longer she can continue to live on her own. It was a bless-ing she could move into the dawdy haus when Adam and Leah's new home was finished and they moved out. But now I don't know if even our dawdy haus is best for her."

"Would you move her into the main house?" Elizabeth knew assisted living was not an option for the Amish.

"I suppose we might have to," Rachel said with a sigh. "Though I know it would upset her to give up her own space."

Elizabeth suspected that it would be a strain for the rest of the family as well. The Fischer home was large, but with seven of the children still living at home, it was already packed full. They talked about how they might make it work and about

Rachel's struggle to be patient with her mother-in-law. "She is still very good at quilting," Rachel said. "And it makes her happy. We try to keep her stocked with scraps and supplies as much as possible."

"It must be nice," Elizabeth said. "To make something beautiful and useful like that." Mama had tried to teach Elizabeth to sew when she'd been in high school, but she'd gotten hopelessly confused and given up.

"It is very satisfying," Rachel said. "I could teach you. You could join in our weekly gathering."

"I don't know," Elizabeth said. But the idea was appealing. "Maybe someday."

Soon they pulled into the driveway of the Mast house. The house stood to the right, and the barn to the back, while the furniture store stood close to the road. They parked in a spot near the store and climbed out, and as they walked toward the shop, a woman in Amish dress emerged from the house and waved.

"*Guder nammidaag,*" she called, coming down the steps. "How lovely to see you."

Rachel waved, and when Roseanna got closer, she answered her in Pennsylvania Dutch. Elizabeth gathered they were saying something about a cake, but she wasn't sure what else they were talking about.

"I am sorry, Elizabeth." Rachel must have seen her confusion. "We are being rude. I had asked Roseanna for the recipe for the coffee cake she brought to a gathering last week, and she was telling me she'd written it down." She turned to Roseanna, a hefty woman whose brown hair was threaded with gray. "This is Roseanna. Roseanna Mast, Elizabeth Classen."

"Hallo." Roseanna smiled and waved. "It is nice to meet you. Rachel has told me many things about her favorite neighbors. And I have been meaning to come into your shop. I am so glad you have opened it once again."

"Thank you," Elizabeth said. "It's nice to meet you."

"Abe is in the shop," Roseanna said, gesturing toward the wooden building. "Let us go inside, and he will tell you about what we saw last night."

Rachel led the way into the shop. Just as Elizabeth remembered, the front portion of the building was a showroom, filled with simple but well-made tables, chairs, dressers, and bookshelves. She ran her hand along the smooth surface of a dining table. It looked like walnut, and the joints were so cunningly done she couldn't even see how it was held together. Elizabeth's mind flashed back to the design magazines she'd paged through earlier. There hadn't been one that featured Amish chic, but maybe there should be. The furniture was beautiful in its simplicity. It was less flashy than the orange Saarinen chairs she'd seen featured in one magazine, but that was a good thing, as far as she was concerned.

"Abe," Roseanna called out, and a man with a graying beard emerged from the back of the shop. He wore the traditional black pants and suspenders of the Amish men in this area. "This is Rachel's friend Elizabeth. She would like to know about the car we saw last night."

"Ach. The one that was going too fast?"

The whole place smelled like sawdust, with the oily, earthy tang of some kind of natural finish.

"That is the one," Roseanna said. "Tell them what we saw."

Abe made some kind of grunting noise at the back of his throat, but then he spoke. "We were driving home." He spoke slowly and deliberately, and he wouldn't quite meet Elizabeth's eye, but she was used to that from Amish men. "We were going down the road, and we saw a light coming from the side of the road."

He saw a light? This was the first she'd heard about that.

"Can you tell me about the light?" Elizabeth asked.

"It was just a small light, and it was bouncing up and down. I did not know what it was at first, but Stephen, he is our middle boy, he told me it was a phone."

"Stephen is in his running-around years," Rachel added, explaining to Elizabeth how Stephen would have known about phones.

"I do not know of any phone that lights up and bounces up and down, but Stephen tells me this is because of something called an app."

"That's right. A flashlight app," Elizabeth said. "Was the light blinking?"

"No, not blinking, just going up and down," Roseanna said.

So the phone hadn't been set to SOS when the person was walking, then. When and why had it changed?

"Stephen was explaining that the bouncing came from someone walking as they carried the phone," Abe said.

"Abe did not believe him. He could not understand why someone would be walking down the road at night," Roseanna said.

"What did you think it was?" Elizabeth asked, trying to suppress a smile.

"I did not know." Abe was clearly not amused by his wife's commentary. "But why would someone walk alone down a dark road at night? It does not make sense."

"Maybe they wanted to get some exercise," Roseanna said.

"Humph." Abe made the noise in the back of his throat again, something between a growl and a cough. "I do not understand these Englischers and their exercise. If they would simply work a farm and build things with their hands, there would be no need for these things like jogging and yoga."

Elizabeth was pretty sure that whoever had been carrying the phone down the road had not been doing yoga, but she decided not to go into that. "Maybe the person didn't have a choice. Car trouble," she said, thinking of the car that had been found abandoned earlier. "Or no other way to get where they were going."

He made that noise in his throat again, and then he said, "Whatever the case, from behind us a car came zooming down the road."

"It is very dangerous how fast these cars go down the roads, especially at night," Roseanna said.

Elizabeth nodded. John had indicated Abe had a habit of reporting bad drivers a bit more often than the police thought necessary, but it truly was a problem how fast cars drove on the country back roads. There had been many close calls where a car came zooming over a hill and narrowly missed a slow-moving buggy, and there had been several major accidents in the past few years.

"What kind of car was it?" Elizabeth asked.

"Some kind of truck," Abe said. "I could not tell much beyond that."

So Dylan had been right about that, then.

"It had that Chevy logo on the back. Stephen noticed that," Roseanna said.

"The boy pays far too much attention to cars," Abe said, looking at his wife in a way that communicated that they'd had that discussion before. "I tried to memorize the license plate number of the car as it went past."

"So he could report the car to the police," Roseanna added, almost apologetically. "We do not call the police very often in our community, but after the accidents in the past few years, we have started to report dangerous drivers more."

"That is completely understandable," Elizabeth said.

"But I could not get the whole thing. I only saw the first three letters."

"What were the letters?" Elizabeth asked.

"C-Y-C," Abe said. "But the truck was going too quickly for me to get the rest. Far too quickly for these roads," he added for good measure.

"But tell her what happened after that," Roseanna said.

He looked at his wife for a second before he said, "As the car got closer to the light at the side of the road, it slowed down, and then it pulled over. The flashlight—and I am assuming the person carrying it—moved close to the truck. I guess they were talking. I do not know."

"Could you tell anything about their conversation? Or how the person with the phone seemed to be responding?" Elizabeth asked.

"I could not even see, they were so far down the road."

Elizabeth reminded herself how slowly horses and buggies moved. A distance that would have only taken seconds to cover in a car would take minutes in an Amish buggy. If they had started far enough back that they couldn't see the girl, it made sense that they never got close enough to make out much of what was going on.

"Tell her what happened after that," Roseanna said. Elizabeth wondered why Roseanna didn't just tell her, but she bit her tongue. It was not her place to analyze the dynamics of their marriage.

"Then the light started blinking rapidly and it fell to the ground," Abe said. "It stayed there as the truck zoomed away." He cleared his throat and added, "Still going much too quickly."

"Huh." Elizabeth processed this. The light had started blinking SOS just before the girl got—or was pulled—into the truck. And was left behind when the truck pulled away. "And then the phone just stayed there?"

"It just blinked there by the side of the road," Abe said.

"And we just continued down the road," Roseanna said. Something passed between the husband and wife that Elizabeth couldn't read.

"Did you take a closer look at the blinking light as you went past?" Elizabeth asked tentatively.

"I wanted to," Roseanna said. "In case the person who had left the phone behind needed help. But Abe was worried."

"I did not want to get involved," he said simply.

Neither one of them spoke for a moment. Again, it wasn't her place to make judgments about their marriage, especially as someone who had never been married herself. But she did wonder if Roseanna ever felt a tiny bit stifled.

"I had four children in the buggy," Abe said. "And it was way past Sylvia's bedtime."

There was a pause while they considered this. She could understand his not wanting to put his children in danger, but considering what they had just seen, didn't he want to try to help? Wasn't he the least bit curious about what he'd witnessed?

"So, anyway, we continued on," Roseanna said, seeming to affect a breezy tone.

"But you mentioned it to someone this morning," Elizabeth said.

"Yes, I spoke to Ruth Yutzy, and I suppose she told Esther Detweiler."

"And I heard it from Esther," Rachel said. "And so here we are."

"And here we are, involved," Abe said, his voice sour. It would have been funny if it hadn't been so upsetting.

"I appreciate your willingness to help," Elizabeth said, even though she got the sense it was Roseanna who was really the willing party here.

"Is there anything else you can remember about the incident?" Elizabeth asked. "Anything at all that you remember might be useful."

"That is all I know," Abe said. "Now, I am sorry, but I must go finish the table I am working on."

"Of course," Elizabeth said. "Thank you for your help."

He made the noise in his throat again, and then he turned and headed into the back.

Elizabeth turned to Roseanna, who was looking at Elizabeth with a hopeful smile. She was either used to or unfazed by Abe's grumpiness. Which, she guessed, was a good thing.

"If you had to guess, would you say the girl got into that truck willingly?"

"How do you know that it was a girl?" Roseanna asked.

She was sharper than she'd let on, Elizabeth thought, and wondered if they would get some real answers now that Abe was out of the room.

"We found the phone," Elizabeth said. "The one that dropped at the side of the road. It had a sparkly pink case, so we're just assuming it belonged to a woman."

"Ach." Roseanna nodded. "That does make sense." A pause, and then she continued, "I am sorry we did not stop and try to help. My husband is—" She broke off, and after a nod from Rachel, she continued. "He did not want to get involved."

Elizabeth guessed it wasn't what she had really wanted to say, but it was enough.

"In any case, if I had to guess, I would say no."

It took Elizabeth a moment to catch up to what Roseanna was saying.

"You don't think she got into that truck willingly," Elizabeth clarified.

"No, I do not. The way the car drove off so quickly, and, well, most Englischers, they do not leave their cell phones behind, do they?"

"No." Elizabeth had to agree. "Most people don't leave their cell phones behind willingly."

It was what she had been thinking. They all had. She hadn't been able to stop thinking about the disappearance of Amber Barber ever since she'd found the phone. But still, somehow hearing it from someone who had watched it happen made it so much worse.

She tried to ignore the sense of dread that crept through her.

CHAPTER TEN

Elizabeth called John when they got back to the car. She knew Abe did not want to get involved, but the Mast family members were the only witnesses to what was potentially a dangerous crime, and she didn't feel she could keep it to herself. Not only that, but Abe and Roseanna had confirmed what Martha's grandson Dylan had gathered: the vehicle that had left the tire marks at the scene was a truck. And she now had the first three digits of the license plate. Elizabeth told John everything she'd learned, and he promised to run a search on the license plate and to send a team out to interview the Mast family right away.

"Shall we go visit Alma Yoder next?" Rachel asked from the passenger seat.

Elizabeth had gotten so wrapped up in what she'd discovered that she'd almost forgotten her original task had been to interview the people who had bought linens at the shop last Saturday.

"If you have time." It was edging towards five, but there were still many hours of daylight left.

"I always have to time to visit a friend," Rachel said.

"In that case, that would be great," Elizabeth said. Alma was in Rachel's quilting circle that met at the shop, and Elizabeth had met her a few times, but she knew that Alma

would feel more comfortable—and hopefully freer to speak—
with Rachel there. "Which way?"

Rachel directed her to the Yoder farm, and as Elizabeth drove,
Rachel asked her about the damage from the storm the previous
week. She'd sent her teen boys Luke and Ephraim over to nail
new roof tiles on the day after the storm had passed through, but
she knew there had been damage inside the house too.

"We're going to have to strip the wallpaper," Elizabeth said.
"And Mary has convinced me to take the opportunity to redecorate."

"That could be fun," Rachel said. "What will you do?"

"I don't know," Elizabeth said. "Mary gave me all kinds of
magazines to look at to try to give me some ideas."

"And what did you think?"

Elizabeth sighed. "There are so many beautiful ways to
decorate these days. You can mimic any style, from any time
period, or you can go Danish minimalist or shabby chic or
industrial or bohemian or beach house, or, I don't know. A
million other possibilities."

"Did any of them appeal to you?"

"Yes. Most of them. That's the problem. I think many of them
are beautiful. But I just can't decide if any of them are really me."

Rachel was quiet for a few moments. Elizabeth tried to be
patient while she figured out what she wanted to say.

"You have had a lot of changes in the past year," Rachel
finally said.

Elizabeth turned her head slightly to look at her friend. That
hadn't exactly been where she'd thought Rachel would go with that.

"What do you mean?"

"I mean, with your mother passing and your sisters coming home, it must feel like everything is different than it was a year ago."

"That's true." It wasn't all bad change though. Of course, losing Mama had been awful, but having her sisters home again was like a dream come true.

"And your sisters...Well, they both have strong personalities."

Elizabeth laughed. "That's true too. They are both exactly who they are, and there's no getting around that."

Another pause, one that stretched out just a bit too long to be comfortable. Then Rachel said, "It could be hard to know exactly who you are in the midst of all that."

Elizabeth turned the words over in her mind, trying to understand what Rachel was getting at. Hadn't they been talking about decorating? Why was Rachel talking about her sisters and change?

She started to ask, but Rachel said, "I am sure you will find a look that is just right for you." And then she started chatting about Ephraim, who was struggling with whether to join the church or not. Elizabeth knew he was on *rumspringa*—the running-around years—and was enjoying the freedom to explore the Englisch world, but she also knew that most Amish teenagers did ultimately give it up to join the Amish church. Still, Rachel worried, as any mother would.

When they arrived at Alma Yoder's home, Rachel led her up to the side door and called into the house, "Hallo! Visitors!"

Alma emerged from some back room and laughed when she saw Rachel. She said something in Pennsylvania Dutch, but Elizabeth couldn't pick up on it. All she understood was that Alma seemed delighted to see Rachel. Alma pulled her in for a hug, and then she turned to Elizabeth. "Elizabeth. It is so good to see you." She hugged Elizabeth too. Elizabeth wasn't exactly a huggy person, but she let Alma give her a squeeze and then pull away.

Alma was older than both Elizabeth and Rachel, and nearly as big around as she was tall. "Please, have a seat. I am just making some snickerdoodles for lunch at Susan's tomorrow." Elizabeth wasn't sure who Susan was, but Susan was a lucky woman, judging by how good those cookies looked lined up on cooling racks along the counter.

"Tell me. How is Silas?" Alma asked as she slid a tray of cookies into the oven and set a kitchen timer.

Rachel told her about a problem Silas had been having with his knee—Elizabeth had had no idea about it—as Alma reached up into the cabinet and took down three small plates. She used a spatula to scoop two cookies from the racks onto the plates, and then she slid one in front of Rachel and one in front of Elizabeth and set a third for herself. As Rachel talked, Alma went to the icebox—propane fueled, Elizabeth knew, since the house wasn't wired for electricity—and pulled out a glass bottle of milk. The layer of fresh cream on top made Elizabeth sure the milk had come from the Yoders' cows just that morning. She poured tall glasses for each of them and settled in at the table.

Alma looked at Elizabeth expectantly, but suddenly Elizabeth didn't know where to start. Fortunately, Rachel jumped in.

"Elizabeth is working on a mystery," she said. Elizabeth was touched by the note of pride in her friend's voice.

"Oh yes? I have heard that you and your sisters are quite good at solving mysteries," Alma said.

"I don't know about that," Elizabeth said. "But we do enjoy them. And we had something interesting happen last night."

Elizabeth quickly explained what had happened and how they were trying to track down the owner of the phone and how they believed the abandoned car Martha had seen this morning was related to it.

"So we're trying to talk to each of the people who bought linens from our shop last Saturday," Elizabeth said. "To try to figure out if that person could have any information about the owner of the car or about the owner of the phone."

Alma laughed. "So, you are here to ask me whether I know someone who owns a car or a pink sparkly cell phone?" Her eyes twinkled mischievously. "Or maybe if the phone belongs to me?"

Now that she put it like that, Elizabeth laughed too.

"You know, I have always liked pink," Alma said. "But I am not much for glitter, personally."

Rachel was trying to hold back a smile. The simple wooden furniture and the plain white walls did betray a tendency toward the plain rather than the glittery.

"No, we didn't think the phone might belong to you," Elizabeth said, still smiling. "Though I think glitter would look good on you." She took a bite of cookie, still warm from the oven, and as she chewed she tried to figure out how to rescue herself from this.

"The car then? I have always wanted a little red sports car. Was it a red car?"

"Sadly, no." Elizabeth laughed again. "It was black."

"Oh. Then it definitely does not belong to me." Alma took a sip from her glass. "I only drive red cars."

Elizabeth wondered if she'd ever been behind the wheel of a car at all. Many Amish had not. In any case, they already knew who owned the car.

"I suppose we're more gathering information in this case," Elizabeth said. "So is it fair to say you don't know how a receipt for linens ended up in the front seat of that car?"

"I do not," Alma said. "My husband takes care of our finances, and he files every receipt. He likes to keep track of every penny." She gave Elizabeth a wry smile. "It is quite annoying, truth be told." She popped the rest of the cookie in her mouth, and when she finished chewing, she said, "I am very pleased with the set of towels I bought at the shop though. They were brand-new and a very good price. Even Amos was pleased, and he does not like it when I spend money, ever."

Rachel and Elizabeth both laughed, and then Elizabeth asked, "Do you know anyone named Jack DiNapoli?"

Alma took a sip of her milk, and Elizabeth did the same. It was cold and tasted rich and creamy and full in the way that only fresh, unpasteurized milk could.

"It does not sound like an Amish name."

"Considering that the car is registered to him, I would be surprised if he was Amish. But maybe you know him? Or the name?"

Alma shook her head. "I am sorry. I do not think I am being much help."

"On the contrary, you are a lot of help," Elizabeth said. "Because now I know for certain that I can cross your name off the list. It wasn't your receipt in the car."

"It is too bad," Alma said. "I would like to have a red sports car."

The timer dinged, and she hopped up to pull the tray of cookies out of the oven. As she used a spatula to move the cookies to the cooling rack, they chatted about the jam Alma was planning to make from the berries in her garden, and Elizabeth enjoyed getting to know her better. She was funny and outgoing and laughed a lot.

Elizabeth and Rachel went back out to the car a while later fuller and happier but no closer to finding answers.

"Do you have time for one more stop before we head back?" Elizabeth asked.

"If I go back now, Hannah will ask me to help with the pork rolls," Rachel said. "Let us please make one more stop."

A few minutes later they were knocking on the door of the address Elizabeth had found for Chrissy Henry. It was a small blue house on a rise along a rural road. A chicken coop stood off to one side of the house, and there was a small farm stand with Fresh Eggs painted on a board next to a blue cooler. Elizabeth wasn't sure if she'd ever met Chrissy Henry, and she was surprised to see a woman with gray curls answer the door. She knew it was silly, but Chrissy sounded like a name for a younger woman.

"Hi." She looked from Elizabeth to Rachel and back again. "If you're selling religion, we don't want it."

Elizabeth was so shocked she wasn't sure how to respond.

But Rachel laughed. "My friend is not Amish," she explained, gesturing to Elizabeth.

What...what was Rachel talking about? Of course Elizabeth wasn't Amish. How could she...What in the world?

"She just prefers to dress plainly," Rachel continued.

Now Elizabeth looked down at her clothes. She was wearing a long tan skirt and a loose gray top. Sure, they were maybe a little baggy, and not exactly the latest style, but it was hardly the standard Amish dress.

Before Elizabeth could protest, Rachel quickly introduced herself and explained that Elizabeth was one of the owners of Secondhand Blessings.

"Oh, right. That cute little shop in the old barn. I like that place." Chrissy's eyes brightened.

Elizabeth tried to recover her words. "We are trying to track down people who bought linens in our shop last Saturday. Our records show that you bought a lace doily, among other things."

"That's right." Chrissy's eyebrow cocked up. "Why?"

Elizabeth tried to figure out how much to say. "We found a cell phone, and we're trying to track down the owner."

"Oh." That seemed to stun her for a moment, and then she stepped back and gestured for them to come inside. Elizabeth followed Rachel in and stopped just inside the doorway.

"Wow." It was all she could get out. The living room was just to the right, and every surface was covered in knickknacks and collectibles. A coffee table was lined with lace and set with dozens of ceramic figurines, the mantel was packed with commemorative plates, and the bookshelves were filled to the brim with figurines and geodes and all kinds of things Elizabeth couldn't even begin to name. There were doilies and lace runners under every surface.

"I see you're a collector." It was all she could get out.

Chrissy nodded, a broad smile on her face. "I have been collecting most of these for decades. I searched for years for some of these."

"They are lovely," Rachel said. "You must be quite proud."

That was what Elizabeth should have said. She knew that none of this was to Rachel's taste, but she made it sound convincing, with so much genuine warmth.

"I do enjoy it." She gestured for them to sit on the light blue couch. Lace antimacassars lay on each armrest, and there was an intricate lace doily draped on the back of the couch. Elizabeth moved toward it hesitantly, but Rachel strode across the room and sat down confidently. Chrissy sat down in a tufted armchair.

"So. You said you found a phone?"

"Yes." Elizabeth lowered herself onto the couch. It was springy but surprisingly comfortable. "We found a cell phone, in a pink sparkly case, and we think it is related to someone who bought linens at our shop last Saturday."

"Hmm." Chrissy turned her head to consider this. "I have my phone." She pulled it out of her pocket, and Elizabeth saw that it was an old-fashioned flip phone. "But my great-niece lost hers a few days ago. It could be hers."

"This phone was just found—" But before Elizabeth could get more words out, Chrissy had whipped open her phone and was placing a call. Who was she calling, Elizabeth wondered, if her niece's phone was gone?

"This phone was lost just last night," Rachel said. "If your niece lost—"

"Hi, Marsha? Did Makayla ever find her phone?" Chrissy asked. "I've got some ladies here who think they may have found it."

"We don't know that—" Elizabeth began, but Chrissy wasn't listening.

"She did what? You've got to be— Well, if she was my kid— Okay, okay. Right. I'm sure you know exactly how to handle it, just like you always do."

After a pause, where Elizabeth could hear someone talking in a very animated way on the other end of the line, Chrissy said, "I'll talk to you later."

She closed the phone and shook her head. "My sister is raising her grandkids, and she is far too lenient." She blew out a breath. "She's repeating the same bad patterns that led to her daughter going off the rails. But what do I know?"

Elizabeth didn't know how to respond, but Rachel very tactfully spoke up. "I am guessing the phone did not belong to your great-niece?"

"No, apparently she had left it at her boyfriend's house. She knew where it was, she just didn't want to tell Marsha because she knew she'd get in trouble. He's quite a bit older." She gave them a knowing look, and Elizabeth had no idea what to say, but she smiled and apparently that was good enough for Chrissy, who continued. "Boyfriend. Can you believe it? Fifteen and going around with a senior in high school. She's going to end up just like her mother—"

"Do you have any other ideas about who the phone might belong to?" Rachel asked.

Chrissy thought for a moment. "No. I mean, I could see if it belongs to my other sister, but I don't think she—" She opened the phone and started scrolling through the names.

"That's okay," Elizabeth said quickly. She did not want a repeat of that uncomfortable conversation. "We're also hoping to find information about a car. Do you know anyone who drives an old black Camaro?"

She closed the phone and then opened it again absently. "I think Gladys from my church does. I could call her and see if—"

"No, that's all right," Elizabeth said. "Unless you know how your receipt from our shop could have ended up in her car, that doesn't seem necessary."

"No, I don't see how it could have," Chrissy said. "I don't know what happened to it, but I probably tossed it in the trash. That's what I do with most of them."

Truthfully, Elizabeth did the same most of the time, unless it was an important or expensive purchase.

"It was this one over here," Chrissy said, letting out a groan as she pushed herself up. She walked over to the bookcase by the fireplace and pointed to a doily underneath a collection of Precious Moments figurines. Elizabeth wasn't sure how she could keep them all straight.

"It's lovely," Rachel said, which seemed to satisfy Chrissy.

"It is a nice one, isn't it? I almost couldn't believe how cheap it was, but I wasn't going to argue."

Elizabeth smiled, once again unsure of how to respond. She waited a moment, and then asked, "Do you know anyone by the name of Jack DiNapoli?"

"No, I don't think so." Chrissy started to walk back toward the couch. "I could ask my sister. She knows a lot of people."

"No, there's no need of that," Elizabeth said, and pushed herself up. "Just one more question. We're looking for a pickup truck with a license plate that starts with C-Y-C. Do you know anyone who drives one of those?"

Chrissy tilted her head, and one of her dangly gold earrings hit her shoulder. "No, I don't think so."

Before she could offer to call anyone to check, Elizabeth quickly said, "We really thank you for your help."

"It was kind of you to help us," Rachel said and also stood.

"I'm glad I could help." Chrissy really did seem pleased, Elizabeth thought as she led them to the door. Elizabeth gave Chrissy her cell phone number and asked her to call if she thought of anything else that might be relevant.

"I hope to see you back at the store again soon," Elizabeth said, and they waved as they walked out.

As soon as they were back in the car, Elizabeth let out a long breath.

"I do not think she is involved," Rachel said. "Do you?"

"No," Elizabeth said. "She seemed genuine. And she seemed to want to help. Maybe a little too much."

Rachel smiled but said nothing. Elizabeth knew her friend tried to not say anything unkind, and not for the first time she wished she had as much restraint.

Elizabeth started the engine and turned the car around in the driveway. She pulled out onto the road and glanced over at her friend. Rachel was smiling, her lips pressed together tightly.

"What is it?" Elizabeth asked.

Rachel hesitated a moment before she said, "You were looking for ideas for decorating your room. I was wondering if you had taken any cues from what you saw in there."

Elizabeth let out a laugh. "I have never seen so many knick-knacks in my life." After a moment, she added, "They seem to give her joy, so I'm glad for her, but they are not my style."

"That is too bad. I had hoped our visit would have provided you with inspiration." Rachel was biting back a smile.

Elizabeth was once again grateful for her friend. Many people thought the Amish did not have a sense of humor, but like many preconceptions people had about the Amish, it was far from reality. Rachel and Elizabeth chatted about the visit as they drove back toward the Fischer farm, but with every mile, Elizabeth realized the sad truth: She was no closer to finding out what had happened to the girl with the pink phone once she'd gotten into that pickup truck.

CHAPTER ELEVEN

Martha looked around the kitchen with a satisfied sigh. It was a complete disaster, with dishes and bowls of leftovers piled on every surface. It would take ages to clean it all up. But she loved cooking for her family, and if that meant there were a few dishes to clean up, she wasn't about to complain.

"That meat loaf was delicious, Mom," Craig said as he carried the empty baking dish from the table. "What kind of magic did you put in there?"

"No magic, I'm afraid," Martha said. "Just a lot of flavor." She took the dish from Craig and scraped the last little bits of meat into the garbage can.

"I'd love to get the recipe," Molly said as she gathered up the cloth napkins. "The boys don't gobble up my meat loaf like that."

"I'd be happy to share it," Martha said. "It was my daddy's favorite, and I know Craig always loved it too." Secretly she doubted Molly would add all the ingredients the recipe called for, since she was always looking for ways to make recipes healthier, substituting maple syrup for sugar and almond flour for real flour. Martha liked to be healthy, but she didn't have much patience for all that. It was meat loaf. It wasn't supposed to be good for you.

"And these green beans were delicious," Molly said. "They taste so fresh. It's amazing."

"They *are* fresh." Martha squirted dish soap into the baking pan and ran hot water into it. "We picked them up at the farmers' market this afternoon. Next summer I hope we'll have some from our own garden."

"Oh, man." Molly tossed the napkins into the bin in the laundry room and reappeared in the kitchen. "I wish I could have a garden. It's so lovely to think of growing your own food. And think how much money we would save." She glanced at her husband with a smile.

"Remind me. Does chicken grow on plants?" Craig smiled as he started stacking the plates into the dishwasher.

"A few more vegetables in your diet would be good for you." Molly moved back to the table and started gathering up place mats. And then she said to Martha, "Did he always complain about eating vegetables?"

"Always. I tried so hard to get him to eat his veggies, and his brother Kyle absolutely loved them, but it was always a struggle with this one." She elbowed Craig gently. "But you should start a garden if you want one. Why couldn't you?"

"Oh, I don't have time to keep it up," Molly said as she stacked the place mats. "They just take so much maintenance, and we're always busy rushing from school to soccer practice to piano lessons. Maybe in a few years when things calm down a bit."

Martha thought about how things hadn't changed much since she raised her children. She and Chuck had gone against the norm by limiting after-school activities, clubs, and sports.

She still didn't understand why young families felt they had to do everything, but she saw it with all her adult children and most of the families at church. They were constantly moving from one thing to another, and they were so busy they never seemed to have time to enjoy each other. But she knew better than to say that, so instead she asked Molly, "How is work going? Has it slowed down at all?"

"No." Molly sighed. "It never does. It's a busy time of year for us, but it's good." Molly was a lawyer for a nonprofit that represented parents fighting for custody of their children. It was good work, and she cared about it passionately.

Martha looked at Kevin, still sitting at the table, head bowed and thumbs flying. He hadn't been disruptive at dinner, she thought as she set another plate in the dishwasher. Quite the opposite, in fact. He'd been totally checked out, sneaking peeks at his phone in his lap the entire time.

"When did Kevin get his cell phone?" she asked. Both Craig and Molly turned to her, confused, and she realized that they hadn't followed the rabbit trail in her head.

"He seems to be very absorbed in it," Martha explained. "I just wondered if it was new."

"Oh, he's been like that since he got it," Molly said. "About two months ago."

"It's funny, because he doesn't seem like he has that many friends." Craig grabbed the dish towel hanging from the oven door and started wiping down the counters. "But the second he got the phone, he started chatting with them nonstop. We realized it wasn't that he didn't have friends, it's just that kids these days interact with their friends very differently than we did."

"Does he ever see his friends in real life? Or do they just text each other?" Martha asked.

"Oh, they see each other in school," Molly said, "But they're all so busy with after-school activities and whatnot that they don't really have time to just hang out like we did. So this is how they stay in touch. It's just different."

Yes, Martha thought. It was indeed different. But was it better? She couldn't help but think something was lost if they weren't seeing each other face-to-face. Spending time with a friend was a whole different thing than chatting via phone.

"Plus, to be honest, it's so much safer," Molly said. "We never have to worry about where they are, like our parents did when we were kids. He's always got his phone on him, so we can track his location, and if worse comes to worst, we can call him."

Martha pressed her lips together to avoid saying the wrong thing. She needed to tread carefully here. "I guess I hadn't thought about the safety issue," she said slowly.

When Craig was Kevin's age, he and the other boys in the neighborhood had vanished into the woods behind the house on the little cul-de-sac for hours. Martha had never been sure where they were, and they didn't have cell phones to track their children back then. But Craig had always made it home in time for dinner, and he talked about the games they had played and the forts they had built and the adventures they had created. Martha hadn't ever worried about his safety, not really. But these days it seemed like parents were always so worried about the dangers all around their children that they weren't allowed to have any freedom at all. Martha had read that in fact the rate of crimes like kidnapping—every parent's worst nightmare—had gone way down.

Then again, she thought with a start, there was a strong possibility a girl had been kidnapped just last night, just a few miles from here.

Martha set another plate in the dishwasher and decided to try another approach.

"Do you usually allow him to use his phone at the dinner table?"

She saw a glance pass between Molly and Craig. What did that mean?

"No, Mom, he's not usually allowed to use his phone at the table," Craig said. Something in his voice sounded strained.

But Kevin had been using it tonight. Surely they had seen that?

"He's on it quite a lot," Martha said instead, hoping that using generalities would deflect any defensiveness they might feel at her questions.

"He is," Molly said. There was a note of exaggerated patience in her voice. "And we have talked to him about that. But he gets so upset when we tell him to put the phone away that it's sometimes not worth the fight. Tonight seemed like one of those times."

Martha rolled her words around in her head before she responded. *So what if he gets upset?* she wanted to say. *You're the grown-ups, and you set the rules. Let him be upset.* But she knew from experience that very few things could cause a rift between herself and her son and daughter-in-law like a perceived slight about their parenting. Martha had always liked Molly, and even though Molly and Craig's quick engagement their senior year of college and the birth of Kevin six months later hadn't been Martha's dream for her son, she was always grateful that Craig had ended up with a strong, smart, kind woman who genuinely loved him. And for the most part, Martha and Molly had gotten along, but there had been a couple of misunderstandings through the years, often after Martha had made a suggestion about her grandchildren.

"I'm glad he's making connections," she said carefully. "But I would love to see a bit more of his face while he's here."

Another glance between Molly and Craig. Some wordless communication that they both understood, and that no doubt had to do with her. Had she crossed a line? But she'd just said she wanted to enjoy her grandson's visit. How could that have been offensive?

"Yes, Mom," Craig said. "Message received."

"We'll talk to him about it," Molly said.

But neither one of them was happy about it, that was clear.

Martha wasn't sure what to say, so they ended up cleaning up the rest of the kitchen in silence.

Elizabeth found Mary curled up in a wingback chair reading when she went upstairs that evening. Craig and Molly had gone up to the guest room shortly after they'd cleaned up from dinner, and the lights were on in the attic where Dylan and Kevin were staying, but the room was quiet. Elizabeth was wiped out from the long day, but before she crawled into bed, she wanted to check on Martha, who'd seemed upset after dinner.

She knocked gently on Martha's door, and Martha called for her to come in.

"I just wanted to see if everything was all right," Elizabeth said. She poked her head in, and the smell of roses greeted her. "I noticed things were a little tense after dinner."

"I'm okay," Martha said from the armchair in the corner of the room. She was looking at something on her tablet. "But thank you for checking. It was...I tried to ask Craig and Molly to keep Kevin from looking at his phone so much and to stay in the real world more, at least while he's here, but it didn't exactly go as I'd planned."

"Ah." Elizabeth stepped into the room and pulled the door mostly closed behind her. "I see."

This was Martha's childhood bedroom, but Mama had used it as a sewing room for the past decade or so. Martha had cleaned it out and moved her own bedroom furniture in, and it looked lovely. There was an elaborately carved mahogany sleigh bed piled with rose-colored satin bedding and pillows, and a heavy matching dresser with an attached mirror. The walls were a soft beige, covered with gilt-framed pictures, and the two windows were hung with layers of pink satin drapes and lacy sheers. It was pretty, Elizabeth thought.

"Yes, well, as you can imagine they weren't thrilled, and took it as an indictment of their parenting."

"Oh, Martha. I'm sorry." Martha did have a way of coming across harsher than she intended, and Elizabeth wondered if that's what had happened in her conversation with Craig and Molly. She knew Martha meant well, but sometimes she didn't realize how she sounded. "I am sure they will have forgotten it by morning."

Craig would have, Elizabeth was sure. He had always been a happy-go-lucky kid, and he'd maintained his positive outlook and naturally sunny disposition into adulthood. But Martha sometimes struggled with Molly, Elizabeth knew. Some small part of her thought Martha had never quite forgiven Molly for getting pregnant in college, as if she'd done it somehow to trap Craig into marriage. Elizabeth was nearly certain that the news hadn't come as a pleasant surprise to Molly herself at the time, though it all seemed to have worked out well in the end.

"I hope they haven't forgotten it," Martha said. "I mean, I hope they ask him to put down his phone." She let out a sigh. "But I do hope they aren't mad at me tomorrow."

"I'm sure things will look better in the morning," Elizabeth said. It felt trite, but it was usually true. "I would have thought you'd be in bed by now."

"I intended to be," Martha said. "But I decided to just see if there was any way to figure out who that truck Abe and Roseanna Mast saw belonged to using the first part of the license plate."

"Did you come up with anything?"

Martha shook her head. "No." She gestured for Elizabeth to come forward and take a look. Elizabeth walked to the corner of the room, noticing the tufted velvet upholstery of the armchair where Martha sat and the rose glass hurricane lamp on the Queen Anne side table. It was cozy and warm, and the whole room had a refined, upscale look. Maybe Elizabeth could try incorporating some of these elements into her room.

"I was trying to find information on Jack DiNapoli," Martha said. "Or some way to get in touch with him. But I'm not finding much of anything."

"Yes, I discovered that earlier today," Elizabeth said. The smell of roses intensified as she got closer to the silver dish holding potpourri on the side table. "But John is looking into him, so hopefully he'll come up with answers."

"I hope so." Martha looked back down at her tablet. "So then I tried to find out if there was a way to track all the pickup trucks in the area, or anything like that." She swiped her finger across the screen and opened a browser window.

"Did you find anything?"

"No, sadly. Either they don't track that kind of thing, or it's not public knowledge."

Elizabeth hoped that sort of information wasn't tracked by the government or anyone else. She hated to think that someone or some branch of government might keep track of all kinds of information about their daily lives.

"I suppose that's good," she said gently.

"Yes, I suppose that is, in general," Martha agreed. "But it means I'm not getting us any closer to finding out what happened to that girl."

It was weighing heavily on Elizabeth's mind too. It had now been a full day, and they had learned more about how the phone had been left behind but were no closer to actually finding the girl. It was as if she had vanished. And with every moment that passed, she could be in more trouble.

"I know," Elizabeth said. It was all she could think to say.

"Well, I'm sure things will look brighter in the morning," Martha said. "Someone smart once told me that."

Elizabeth smiled. "I sure hope you're right."

CHAPTER TWELVE

Sunday morning dawned bright and sunny. Elizabeth checked her phone and found a message John had sent at nearly eleven the night before, saying they hadn't found any vehicle of any kind in the area registered with a C-Y-C license plate. Well, that was another dead end, then. She heaved herself out of bed.

The house was quiet, and she made her way downstairs silently, Pal trailing along behind her. She avoided the creaking third step. Craig and Molly were on vacation and would no doubt want to sleep in. She stepped into the kitchen and started the coffee, and soon the rich, earthy scent started to fill the quiet kitchen. Tink, Mary's dachshund, looked up from her spot on the living room rug. Elizabeth slid the back door open, and both dogs bounded into the yard. She watched Pal sniff the fence while Tink circled an elm tree. It was going to be another hot day, she could already tell.

"Hi."

Elizabeth gasped and whirled around and found Dylan standing next to her, a book tucked under his arm. His hair was sticking up in the back, and he wore baggy sweatpants and a Superman T-shirt.

"Good morning, Dylan," she said.

"Sorry. I didn't mean to scare you."

"That's okay." Her heart was pounding so hard it could probably count as aerobic activity. "I just didn't realize anyone else was down here."

"I woke up early." Dylan shrugged. "I always wake up early. Kevin said he would punch me if I kept making noise in our room, so I came down here."

"Sounds like the right call," Elizabeth said.

"I'm hungry," Dylan said. "Can I get something to eat?"

"Of course. What would you like?"

"What do you have?"

"Well, let's see. There's yogurt, or cereal, or eggs." It was Sunday morning, and they had church, but that wasn't for a few more hours. "Or we could make pancakes, or waffles."

"Pancakes." His eyes lit up. "With real flour?"

"Real flour, for sure," Elizabeth agreed. "Let's see. Can you grab the eggs?"

A few minutes later, they had mixed up the batter, and golden round discs were sizzling in the pan. Elizabeth warmed real maple syrup from a local Amish family on the stove, and then she and Dylan sat down to eat. The pancakes were fluffy and warm and delicious, and they each had a second helping before loading their plates in the dishwasher. The house was still quiet. Elizabeth's plan had been to look through those design magazines again, to see if any of them discussed incorporating Victorian touches into a bedroom, like Martha had, but she didn't want to leave the poor kid on his own.

"Would you like to help me feed the animals?" she asked him.

"Yes!" Dylan started hopping up and down. The sugar from the syrup must have kicked in already.

"All right. Go get your shoes."

Dylan helped her gather the eggs and clean the goats' pen. He was a sweet kid, Elizabeth thought. He was often so much in the shadow of his older brother that it was nice to get to spend some time just with him, and they laughed as a goat nibbled on his hair and as he chased poor Reddy the rooster around the yard.

They walked out to the mailbox together and retrieved the Sunday edition of the Lancaster paper from the box just next to the mailbox. She scanned the headlines on the first few pages as they walked back toward the house. The story of the found phone and missing girl was on the lower half of the third page. She skimmed the article, looking for any new information, but the reporter hadn't learned anything Elizabeth hadn't. John was quoted in the article, asking anyone with information about the whereabouts of the owner of the phone to come forward. On one hand, the fact that news of a cell phone being found was in the paper at all spoke to how safe the area really was and how low the crime rate was; on the other hand, it wasn't really a story about a phone being found, it was a story about a girl gone missing.

When they came back in, Molly had come downstairs and was making another batch of pancakes, so Elizabeth headed upstairs to get ready for church. But as she studied her closet, she noticed that she had a missed call on her phone. Goodness. It was barely eight o'clock in the morning. Who would call at this—but maybe it was John with news—

She grabbed the phone and unlocked it but saw that it was an unfamiliar number. There was a voice mail, so Elizabeth held the phone to her hear to listen to the message.

"Hi, Elizabeth, this is Chrissy Henry. You came here yesterday." Elizabeth recognized the voice immediately. "You asked me if I knew anyone who drives a pickup with the license plate that started with C-Y-C. Well, I have a camera set up at the farm stand at the end of my driveway because people keep taking eggs without paying for them. I found out yesterday it happened again, so I was watching the footage from the past few days, and you'll never guess what I saw. A pickup truck went past here Friday night, and when I slowed the footage down I saw that it had a license plate that started with C-Y-G. It's not exactly what you were looking for, but I wondered if it might be the same one. Anyway, give me a call if you want to come take a look."

Elizabeth glanced at the clock. She still had plenty of time before church started.

It was probably nothing, she realized. This area was filled with trucks. It was farm country, after all. What were the chances that Chrissy would happen to have caught the exact pickup they were looking for? And it didn't have the right license plate. But she couldn't simply ignore a lead, no matter how crazy it was.

She quickly called Chrissy back. "This is Elizabeth Classen. Would it be all right if I come now?"

"That would be fine. I'll be here."

By the time Elizabeth got ready to go, Mary had come downstairs, and it didn't take much convincing to get her to come along.

"It sounds like an adventure," she said, pouring coffee into a travel mug.

"What were you reading last night?" Elizabeth asked as they followed the GPS directions to the same blue house she'd visited yesterday.

"It was a book about the history of Lancaster County," Mary said. "It was fascinating. Did you know that the Conestoga wagon was invented here?"

Elizabeth supposed she had learned that at some point in school, but she hadn't remembered that.

"And before European settlers moved in, there were at least half a dozen Native American tribes living here."

"That's very interesting," Elizabeth said. "But why the sudden interest in local history?"

"It's because of that sampler," Mary said with a sigh. "I know it's silly, but it's made me curious about what life would have been like for the girl who made it."

"That's not silly at all." Elizabeth slowed as an Amish buggy appeared on the rise ahead of them. A family on their way to church, she supposed. "It's interesting to think how different her life would have been than the way kids live now." She thought about Kevin, just a year older than Frances would have been. Frances wouldn't have had a cell phone, for one thing, but she thought it probably went much deeper than what material possessions they did or didn't have. A twelve-year-old back then would have been seen as a little adult, she thought, or at the very least on her way to adulthood. The very fact she had made a sampler showed that she was being prepped for the skills she would need in marriage. The idea of

Kevin getting ready for marriage was so funny she almost laughed out loud.

"Have you found anything?" she asked.

"Not much in the way of specifics." Mary took a sip from her coffee. "I did some digging in the genealogical archives at the library yesterday hoping to find out more about her life, and I found out where she was born and when she got married. But the librarian promised to look into it and see what she could find."

"Wow." Elizabeth hadn't realized her sister had taken it that far. It was impressive, in a strange kind of way. But then, Mary always got swept away by things that interested her, and even though she wasn't typically one to spend long hours in a library, it wasn't at all unusual to find her extremely focused on something.

"I just want to see what happened to her," Mary said. "I don't know what it is, but seeing her work... Her personality comes out, don't you think? You can tell she had a very proper upbringing and did what she was expected to do, dotted her i's and crossed her t's. But you can also tell she had a bit of spunk, a bit of spirit, and that if she was going to be forced to do this task, she was going to do it her way."

"The artist in you recognizes the piece of herself she left in her work," Elizabeth said.

"Yes." Mary nodded. "I think that's it exactly."

"It makes sense, then, that you want to learn more about her life."

"I just want to see if she ended up happy," Mary said. "If she found ways to express that spirit she had to hide in a society that didn't exactly encourage girls to stand out and be themselves."

Elizabeth understood Mary's search a little more after hearing her talk about what interested her about it. "I can't wait to see what you find."

"Me neither." Mary smiled and took a sip of her coffee. "Now, tell me what you thought of those magazines I bought for you."

Elizabeth didn't know what to say. "I thought there were a lot of people trying to sell me things," she eventually said.

"Not the ads, silly," Mary said. "I mean, did you find a style that appealed to you? Did any of the pictures seem like anything you would like?"

Elizabeth tried to think back over the pictures she'd seen in the glossy magazine pages, but they all blended together.

"I wasn't a fan of the more modern design," she finally said. "I don't think that's for me." All those sharp angles and mirrored surfaces and horrible dark wood.

"No, I didn't really think it would be," Mary said. "But it was worth looking at it to make sure."

"I suppose it was. And I don't think Victorian is really for me either," Elizabeth said. She hadn't really realized it until the words came out, but it was true. She had appreciated the intricately carved details of the armoires and desks and sideboards that she had seen. Whoever had made that furniture cared about how it looked and took a lot of time to design beautifully turned legs and rounded fronts. It took skill and would look lovely in the right room. But she wasn't as excited about the painted hurricane lamps and the flocked wallpapers and the heavy drapes.

"Martha's room is perfect for her, and I think she would love the magazine that featured that style. But I think it's a bit fussy for me."

"Yes, I suppose that's true," Mary said. "I don't see you going in for lacy doilies and velvet furniture."

Elizabeth did like the elegance the style gave a room. But it didn't really seem like her.

"I think country charm would be more up your alley, personally," Mary said.

"Country charm?" She pictured lots of American flags and wallpaper with chickens on it.

"You know. Farmhouse style. White wood, colorful quilts, lots of wooden furniture and galvanized steel and soft rugs. Haven't you ever seen *Fixer Upper*?"

"I can't say I have." Elizabeth didn't watch much television, but she'd heard of the show. "Isn't that where they take a place that's falling apart and make it look amazing?"

"Yes, basically. And they often give them this beautiful farmhouse style that I think you would love."

It sounded a lot like the style Mary had decorated her room with, honestly. And Mary's room did look nice.

"I'll think about it," Elizabeth said and then turned her focus back to the road. They were almost to Chrissy's house now, and Elizabeth paid attention to the road they were on. It was just a typical country road, she thought, with a mixture of newer houses and stately older homes, a few trailers, a farm or two. She pulled up in front of Chrissy's house, noticing again the farm stand at the end of the driveway. Chrissy met them at the door and ushered them inside. Elizabeth introduced Mary, who refused to meet Elizabeth's eyes as she took in the décor.

Chrissy led them to the woodgrain vinyl-topped table in the kitchen that was covered with stacks of newspapers and piles of old catalogs. She set a laptop down in front of them in the only available space, a place setting that must be where Chrissy ate.

"You said you have a camera set up at the farm stand?" Elizabeth asked as Chrissy lowered herself down onto a caned chair next to them. The kitchen, like the living room, was packed with stuff. Every surface was covered with bottles of spices and canisters of coffee and jars of some kind of leaves Elizabeth couldn't identify.

"Yes. My hens produce more than I need, so I put out fresh eggs just about every day, as well as a few tomatoes or zucchini or whatever I have. It's self-serve, on the honor system, and I've never had a problem until recently. A new family moved in down the road—the place with the Dale Earnhardt Jr. flag flying from that rusted-out car in the yard?"

Elizabeth had seen it as they drove past.

"Well, ever since they moved in, money has been going missing from the till. I'll go out there to collect the cash at the end of the week and find that someone has swiped the whole thing. It's infuriating. I have a fixed income, and I rely on that little bit of money I make. I know it's them, but I couldn't prove it, and when I went down there to tell them to stop, well, they weren't so pleased about that, as you might imagine."

"No doubt," Mary said. She did a good job of conveying sympathy, Elizabeth thought.

"So I set up one of those security cameras," Chrissy said. "The kind you can see from your computer screen. I saw it advertised on TV. Got it when it was on sale at Walmart." She pulled up a grainy black-and-white image of the farm stand and the road in front of it.

"I went out to check this morning, and the cash was gone, so I went through and looked at the camera footage to see if I could catch them in the act."

"Did you?" Mary asked.

"Check this out." Chrissy advanced the footage to an image of a figure in the dark. The picture was hard to make out, though there was some kind of night-vision filter that made it possible to see in the dimly lit night. The person on the screen was wearing a hat, and it was difficult to tell much of anything. But it was clear there was a person there, and the three women watched as he—it had to be a man, Elizabeth thought, though it was hard to say why she thought that—approached the farm stand, opened the cooler, reached in, pulled out a plastic bag, and stuck it in his pocket. It was so quick, and so smooth, that it seemed likely this wasn't his first time raiding the cooler.

"It's too bad you can't really tell anything about him," Elizabeth said. "You can see someone was definitely there, but you couldn't say who it was."

"Sure she can," Mary said. Elizabeth glanced over at her sister. What was she talking about? "His hat," Mary explained.

Chrissy nodded. "Exactly."

"What?" Somehow Chrissy and Mary had seen something she'd totally missed.

"It's the neighbor," Mary said. "See the number on his hat?"

Had there been a number on his hat? Chrissy backed up the footage and showed it again, and this time Elizabeth noticed that there was indeed a number on the hat. She squinted, and it looked like the number 88. Chrissy stopped the footage.

She'd seen that number recently.

"My ex was a Junior fan," Mary said.

That was it. Dale Earnhardt Jr. She'd seen the number 88 on that flag in the neighbor's yard.

"It's them," Elizabeth said.

"Exactly," Chrissy said again. "Now I just have to show this footage to the police. I called them and told them I had proof of a crime, but they didn't seem to be in any big hurry to get here."

"I'm sure they'll come soon," Mary said, her voice soothing the obvious frustration in Chrissy's. "I'm sure they're busy, but they will no doubt take this seriously."

Chrissy's response was somewhere between a grunt and a nod, but it was clear she was mollified that Mary was taking her seriously.

"Now, I almost stopped watching after this point, but my sister Marsha called, and I just let the footage run while I talked to her." Chrissy pressed the space bar to let the footage run once again, this time at double speed. There was no movement aside from the occasional animal scurrying past. After a few minutes with no movement at all, a light appeared at the left side of the screen. It illuminated the road, and it soon became clear that it was from a vehicle's headlights. A dark-colored pickup truck appeared on the screen, and as it went past the camera, Chrissy paused the video. "I saw this, and then I went back and watched it again, to make sure of what I thought I'd seen."

She used the bar at the bottom of the screen to slowly advance the footage a few frames at a time, and she stopped it when the truck's license plate came into view. CYG 7835.

Abe thought the license plate on the truck he'd seen had started with C-Y-C. But it had been nighttime, and he'd seen it from a distance. Was it possible he'd read the plate wrong? *C* and *G* could easily be confused.

Elizabeth had no idea if this was the same pickup that Abe Mast had seen stop for the girl by the side of the road. It would be quite a coincidence; there were pickups everywhere on these back roads. But the license plate number was close enough to the one Abe reported to be intriguing.

"What time was this?" Elizabeth asked.

Chrissy pointed to the time stamp in white digits at the corner of the screen. The truck had driven past just after nine on Friday. That would put it about twenty to thirty minutes after Abe had seen it stop and pick up the girl by the side of the road. Elizabeth pictured the roads in her head. Yes, this was close enough to where the girl had been picked up that it could have made it here by this time.

She glanced at Mary, who was nodding. It was possible.

"This was Friday. You didn't check the footage until this morning?" Elizabeth tried to understand. If Chrissy was all that concerned about the egg money, it seemed likely she would have checked it sooner.

"I didn't have a chance to go out to the farm stand yesterday, so I didn't realize the money was gone until this morning," Chrissy said.

"May I?" Elizabeth pointed to the bar at the bottom of the screen.

"Have at it," Chrissy said.

Elizabeth backed the footage up and watched the truck come into view from the left side of the screen once again. There was the dark shape of a person sitting in the driver's seat, but she couldn't tell anything about the person. The passenger seat was empty.

"Have you ever seen this truck before?" Mary asked.

"Not that I remember. But lots of people live along this road, and I don't necessarily know what everyone drives," Chrissy said. "It could be nothing, but, you know, since you'd asked about a truck with a plate like that, I thought it made sense to let you know."

"I'm so glad you did." Elizabeth made a note of the license plate number and the make of the truck—it was a Chevy Silverado, according to the markings on the tail— and thanked Chrissy for calling. One of Roseanna's children, the one on rumspringa, had mentioned a Chevy logo on the truck they'd seen. Her heartbeat sped up. This really could be connected.

When they were back in the car, Elizabeth gave John a call, explaining what they'd seen.

"That's an interesting possibility," John said to her suggestion that Abe had read the license plate wrong. "I can run a search for the full plate number of the truck in the footage and see if anything turns up on that one. We can at least find out who it's registered to and see what they can tell us about Friday night."

It was the first note of hope she'd had all morning.

CHAPTER THIRTEEN

I'm sorry, I'm sorry. I'm ready now." Mary hurried down the stairs, holding up her skirt so she didn't trip. How did Elizabeth always get ready so quickly? Even when she was trying to hurry, Mary ended up taking twice as long as her sister.

"You look nice." Elizabeth looked up from—was that a road map?—and smiled. She had a cup of coffee in a handmade ceramic mug next to the map.

"Thanks." Mary had been going for cool, so she'd selected a sleeveless blouse over a broomstick skirt in a bright floral pattern. "Ready to go?"

Craig and Molly and the kids were rushing around upstairs, trying to get ready to go to church in Martha's car, while Mary was riding with Elizabeth, who probably would have left at least ten minutes ago if she'd been on her own.

"I guess so." Elizabeth started to push herself up, but she seemed reluctant to leave the map behind. Where had she even gotten a road map? Mary hadn't seen one of those in years.

"What are you doing?" Mary stepped closer and saw that it was a map of the area where they lived, and her sister had marked a couple of places with a yellow highlighter.

"I tried to map it out," Elizabeth said. "To see if it made sense."

"The phone?" Mary understood now.

"Exactly." Elizabeth pointed to a spot she'd marked on the map. "This is where we found the phone."

Mary nodded, peering down at the spot on the map. It was a few miles from their farmhouse, on one of the country roads that threaded through the fields and farmlands.

"It lines up pretty exactly with where Abe Mast says he saw the car pull over and the phone fall."

Mary shuddered, thinking about what it must have been like to witness that. She knew they didn't have any proof that what had happened Friday night was like the kidnapping of Amber Barber. But Mary couldn't shake the feeling they were linked, or at least similar.

"And here's where Martha saw that abandoned car." Elizabeth traced her finger along a road just south of where the girl had been last seen.

It was hard to tell distances on this map, but Mary guessed it was about half a mile from where the phone had been found.

"Her car broke down," Mary said. "And she was walking...where?"

"Somewhere over here," Elizabeth said, indicating the huge area to the north and east of the spot. "And then this is where the truck showed up on the security camera."

The spot she'd marked was a few miles to the east.

"You don't know if it's the same truck," Mary said.

"No, we don't," Elizabeth agreed. "It's very possible it has nothing to do with this. But since John didn't find a truck with a C-Y-C plate, he's looking into whether there's any chance the truck from the footage could be it. And if it is, then the truck had to get from here"—she pointed to the spot where the phone had been found and the girl had been seen getting into the truck—"at about eight forty, to here"—she pointed to the spot where Chrissy's farm stand security camera had captured the image of the license plate—"at just after nine."

"So about twenty minutes."

"Right."

Mary tried to picture the distance in her mind. "It's not very far, really."

"It's just under five miles," Elizabeth said. She gestured at the ruler next to the map. "According to the scale on the side of the map."

Goodness. It had been ages since Mary had measured distances by measuring on a map. Why hadn't Elizabeth just popped it into Google Maps?

"He should have gotten a lot farther than five miles in that time," Mary said. On these back roads, people rarely drove below forty miles per hour, and usually well above that. He should have been able to get much farther than five miles in twenty minutes.

"Unless he made a stop somewhere," Elizabeth said.

"Right." Mary lowered herself into the spindle-backed chair across from her sister. Mary knew she didn't need to suggest to Elizabeth what might have happened during that stop. She didn't even want to think about it. Whatever had happened to Amber—

"You referred to the truck driver as a 'he,'" Elizabeth said. "I have been assuming it's a man too."

"Aren't kidnappers always men?" It seemed obvious to Mary.

"I have no idea, actually. I would guess statistically they probably are more likely to be men, but I'm sure women commit the crime as well."

She was starting to sound like Martha, talking about statistics. Mary didn't know about statistics. She just knew someone was missing.

"Surely if a woman kidnaps someone, she does it for different reasons. I bet those people who snatch babies to love them and raise them are women," Mary said, and then realized how silly she sounded. It was not any better to snatch a baby than to snatch a girl from the side of the road, no matter what the motivation.

"I don't know," Elizabeth said. "I suppose we don't even really know that she was snatched. Maybe something else entirely happened."

"So you think she just set her phone to blink SOS and then left it behind because she was excited to hop into that truck?" Mary didn't mean to be sarcastic, but somehow it had crept into her voice.

"I wish I knew what I thought." Elizabeth took a sip of coffee. "But I guess you're right. It does seem unlikely that our girl turned on an SOS signal and then left her phone behind if she went willingly. I mean, I guess if we're going to go down that road, we don't know for sure that the person who had the phone was a woman." Elizabeth took another sip, draining the cup.

"It would have to be a very secure man to carry around a phone in a sparkly pink case," Mary said.

Elizabeth sighed. "You're right, of course. I just don't want us to limit ourselves by making false assumptions."

"I think that's smart." Mary hitched her purse up on her shoulder. "But for now, if we don't get going, we're going to be late."

Elizabeth pushed herself up and tried to smile, but Mary could see the worry in her eyes.

Martha let herself relax against the wooden pew. Craig and Molly were sitting just to her left, with Dylan and Kevin just beyond them, and Mary and Elizabeth were at the far end of the pew. The boys were both wearing black dress pants and shiny leather shoes with polo shirts so new they still had the original creases on the sleeves. Craig wore a polo over khakis, and Molly was in a sundress that was lovely. Martha wondered if the family's clothes had been bought specifically for this trip to church. Still, they were here, and that was all that mattered.

Pastor Nagle stepped up to the pulpit, and a hush fell over the room. He announced the first song, number 357, and Martha grabbed the red hymnal from the pew in front of her. "O God, Our Help in Ages Past." One of the finest, Martha had always thought. She glanced down the row and noticed that the boys seemed to have no idea how a hymnal worked. Kevin was flipping pages back and forth, and Dylan was looking through the bulletin, searching for the words, no doubt. Craig finally leaned over and opened the books to the right pages for each of them, and they joined in the song. Martha watched them out of the corner of her eye. She thought there was a decent chance Kevin was simply saying *watermelon* over and over, but she couldn't be sure.

After the song, the congregation sat back down, and it took a moment before Molly and the boys realized they were supposed to sit too. She glanced at Craig. He'd never come out and said that his family didn't attend church regularly, but Martha had suspected it for a while, and now she thought it even more likely. Maybe their church was the more modern kind that projected songs onto screens, she reasoned. But the boys seemed to have no real idea what they were supposed to do when the pastor asked the congregation to bow their heads in prayer.

Still, she thought, settling back into the pew, they were here, and they were with her, and that was all that mattered. After announcements and another song, Pastor Nagle stepped up to the lectern and started to preach on John 10—the parable of the Good Shepherd. One of the classics. Martha listened as he elaborated on the familiar passage, talking about the life of a shepherd in biblical times, bringing context to the verses in a way she'd never heard before. It was enlightening, and soothing, and...wait. Was that...?

She caught something—a brief flash—out of the corner of her eye, and she looked again to make sure she'd seen correctly. Was Kevin...texting? In the middle of the service?

He was looking down at his phone, typing on the little screen. Martha watched him, but he didn't notice her staring at him.

He didn't even seem to be hiding it.

Molly must have noticed Martha's frustration, because she glanced down at her son and quickly took the phone from

Kevin's hands. He started to protest, and she shushed him, and when he argued, she whispered something into his ear. He crossed his arms over his chest and slumped down in his seat.

Molly tucked the phone into her purse and then glanced at Martha. Martha smiled, but she couldn't read the look on Molly's face. It was something like embarrassment, tinged with frustration, and also something she couldn't understand.

Martha tried to focus on the sermon once again, but she couldn't make her mind take in the words. The peace and contentment she'd felt just a few minutes ago had been shattered.

Elizabeth's phone buzzed during the last hymn of the service. She was grateful she'd turned it to silent, and as she reached into her purse, which was sitting on the pew next to her, she snuck a glance at the screen. John. Elizabeth felt a slight pang of disappointment that John was working instead of in church, but she brushed it aside. John was a good man, but he didn't know the Lord, and she would continue to pray for him, that God would draw John to Himself in His own time. For now, Elizabeth hoped that he was calling with some good news. She tucked the phone back into her purse and turned back to the hymnal, though she knew the words to "Fairest Lord Jesus" with her eyes closed.

After Pastor Nagle offered a blessing, they all filed out to the fellowship hall. Susan Reynolds had volunteered for coffee hour again, and she had gone all out. Deviled eggs and zucchini bread and blueberry muffins and a cracker and cheese platter on top of the usual coffee and fruit. The kids seemed to be enjoying it, but Elizabeth had to restrain herself from piling a plate full of sweets. Instead, she carried her phone out into the side yard, overlooking the cemetery where so many members of her family had been buried, and listened to John's voice mail.

"Hi, Elizabeth, it's John. I guess you're probably at church now. I don't know what time you get done there, but I wanted to let you know that I traced the owner of the truck you found the license plate for. Call me back, and I'll give you an update."

Elizabeth called him back right away, and John picked up quickly.

"Hi there," John said. "Done with church?"

"It just ended," Elizabeth said. "And I got your voice mail. You found the truck owner?"

"Yes. The truck on that security footage is registered to a man named Walt Goodwin."

"Walt Goodwin?" Why did that name sound familiar? She closed her eyes and thought for a minute. "Wait. I think my dad was friends with someone named Walt Goodwin."

She thought for a moment more. Daddy had collected antique tractors—a hobby that had driven Mama mad, as she thought all the tractor parts lying around had made the place look junky. Elizabeth was pretty sure Walt was someone he'd met at the Grange Hall who was also into tractors. An image of a tall man with a round belly came into her mind. He had dark hair and a mustache, and he had seemed jolly and kind the few times Elizabeth had met him. But that had been a long time ago. Daddy had been gone for ten years now, and she hadn't thought of Walt in all that time. Surely he couldn't be wrapped up in all this, could he?

"Well..." John hesitated. "I was planning to head out to talk to him. In most cases, I wouldn't suggest bringing a civilian along, but if you know him, I wonder if he might be more willing to talk if you were there."

"I imagine he would." It wasn't that the people around here were unfriendly—quite the opposite, in fact. But most people would be hesitant if a police officer showed up and started asking about their whereabouts on a given night.

"Well, in that case, do you want to come along with me?"

"I would love to. When are you going?"

"I'm just about to head out from the station. As it turns out, the address the truck is registered to is not that far from your place. How about if I swing by and pick you up on the way?"

"That would be great." Mary had plans to go to lunch with a woman she'd met volunteering at the Fourth of July pancake breakfast, and could get a ride home with her afterward. "I'll head home now, and I'll see you in a little bit."

"See you soon."

Elizabeth headed back into the fellowship hall and told Mary what she was doing. Elizabeth had attended Mount Zion Mennonite Church for most of her life, and she knew just about everybody in the room. Most Sundays she enjoyed catching up with friends and neighbors. But she knew she had to move today if she didn't want to keep John waiting, so she walked quickly out the back door and hurried to the parking lot. Martha was planning a big family meal back at the house, so it would be good for Elizabeth to be out of her hair anyway.

She had time to make herself a ham and cheese sandwich and eat it quickly before John's police cruiser pulled into the driveway. Pal ran to the front window to see who had arrived, pressing his nose against the glass. Elizabeth went out to the porch, pulling the door closed behind her, and waved to John just as he stepped out of the car. Her heartbeat sped up at the sight of him in his uniform, though she reminded herself once again that they were just friends.

"You look nice," John said.

"Oh. This?" Elizabeth was still wearing a long blue dress in a light, fluttery fabric. She supposed it was a bit dressier than her everyday outfits. "I didn't change after church."

"I like it." John smiled and walked around to the passenger side of the car and opened the door. The leather seat was surprisingly comfortable, and the air conditioning felt heavenly. "How was church?" he asked as he settled into the driver's seat.

"It was very nice." Elizabeth pulled the seat belt across her lap and buckled it. "Pastor Nagle preached about the Good Shepherd."

"A classic," John said. "'I am the good shepherd; I know my sheep and my sheep know me—just as the Father knows me and I know the Father—and I lay down my life for the sheep.'"

Elizabeth knew she shouldn't be surprised. She knew that John's reluctance to attend church wasn't because he was unfamiliar with religious tradition, but because he had decided he had been forced to attend churches with some questionable teachings as a child and had decided he didn't believe what they taught. But she still couldn't help being just a tiny bit astonished. She wasn't sure she would have been able to quote the passage from John, and she'd just heard it read this morning.

"It was a very nice service," Elizabeth said again. She resisted the urge to invite him to come with her next week. She'd invited him several times, and he'd always declined. He knew the invitation was outstanding. "And how was your morning?"

"Frustrating, for the most part." John backed the police cruiser up and turned it around in the driveway. "We tracked down a phone number and address in State College for Jack DiNapoli, but so far he's not answering his phone. A couple of troopers are going to drive out there this afternoon and try to talk with him, but so far there's not much headway on that front."

"That's distressing."

"And another text came in from Viv on the cell phone. This one said 'I guess you're not coming after all but it sure would have been nice to know that.'"

"What does that mean?" Elizabeth asked.

John shrugged. "It sounds like our girl was expected but never showed up. But we don't know where, or who Viv is. And we still haven't been able to get the phone unlocked."

"None of the combinations you've tried have worked?"

"No. At this point, every time we guess wrong, it locks us out for a longer period of time. And we're worried that it might be set to erase all the information on the phone after ten failed attempts, so we don't want to get there."

John pulled out into the road, and they turned east, toward the town of Intercourse.

"Isn't there some official way to find out how to unlock it?" Elizabeth asked. "Like, can't you make the phone company unlock it for you, or something? I would have thought that for law enforcement, there would be a way to make the phone companies give you that information."

"That's actually a hotly debated topic right now," John said. "There have been some high-profile cases where law enforcement wanted to get into the phone of a suspect—remember the shooting in San Bernardino some years back?"

Elizabeth nodded. She remembered the horrific incident where a man and his wife had opened fire on his coworkers at the company's holiday party.

"The police suspected that information about the planned shooting was on the suspect's phone, but they couldn't get it unlocked, and the shooter was dead. The FBI tried to force the phone manufacturer to unlock it for them, but they wouldn't, on the grounds that they couldn't give away their customer's data."

"Didn't they offer a reward to any hacker who could get the phone open?" Elizabeth asked.

"That's right," John said. "And they did get it open in the end, but it unleashed a lot of debate about privacy and Fifth Amendment rights and when a company must hand over private information about its customers."

"It seems to me that in the case of a mass shooting, the phone manufacturer should want to provide any information they could give the FBI," Elizabeth said.

They were headed back in the same direction she'd gone this morning, toward Chrissy's house.

"I agree," John said. "But it does raise the legitimate question of consumer privacy and who owns the right to share your data. Who is allowed to see what websites you visit and where you spend your money and who you talk to? Some recent court cases have decided that in cases where a phone has a fingerprint recognition technology, the police can force a suspect to use his fingerprint to unlock his phone."

Elizabeth didn't have anything to hide—in some ways, she would be perfectly fine with the government or anyone else seeing the perfectly ordinary and boring things she did online. But she saw the larger point that if you used technology with an expectation that your data would be private, it was hardly fair for the government to gain access to it against your will.

"But none of this is really relevant in this case," John said. "In this case, even if we did get Apple to tell us how to open it, we wouldn't be able to tell them who it belonged to or what phone number's records to pull."

"Right," Elizabeth said. There was that.

"There is newer technology that allows law enforcement to get access to locked phones, but it's very expensive, and our small department doesn't have access to it," John said. "Though we're looking into working with other forces in the area who do have it." He sighed. "But technically, breaking into a phone that way requires a search warrant, and the girl who dropped her phone isn't a suspect, so we probably wouldn't be able to get a warrant in any case."

Elizabeth shook her head. There were so many complexities of the law that she hadn't considered.

"But the most important question isn't how to get the phone unlocked, it's what happened to the girl who dropped it on Friday night, and who is she," John continued. "The phone would possibly be really useful in answering the second question, but the first is the more pressing one." John turned his head so he could see Elizabeth more clearly. "And so far, you and your sisters have been doing a great job helping us try to answer that question."

"I don't know about that. I can't really imagine Walt Goodwin having anything to do with this," Elizabeth said. "So I fear giving you that license plate number may have sent you on a wild-goose chase."

"Tell me what you know about him."

Elizabeth explained that Walt had been a friend of her father's and about their shared love of antique tractors. "My dad was especially fond of John Deeres. I don't know if Walt Goodwin had a favorite or if he just liked all antique models."

"I guess we'll find out," John said. "Do you know anything else about him?"

"His wife always seemed nice. I don't remember her name, but she had long brown hair that I thought was beautiful. She made this really delicious spaghetti one time." She turned and cracked a smile. "Is that the kind of detail that's useful in cases like this? How good the suspect's wife's spaghetti is?"

"I have yet to see spaghetti play a crucial role in a criminal case, but I'm not ruling it out," John said with a grin. "You never know what might turn out to be important."

Elizabeth knew he was mostly joking with her, though there was an element of truth in what he said.

"I think they had a couple of kids and maybe some grand-kids," Elizabeth continued. "They went to the Methodist church over in Lancaster. He was a deacon, or something."

Elizabeth tried to think back, but she couldn't recall anything more about a man she'd only met a few times. "He doesn't sound like your typical kidnapper, does he?"

"No, I suppose not," John said, braking as they approached a stop sign. "Then again, I'm not exactly sure what a typical kidnapper is like."

Elizabeth supposed she didn't know either, but it was hard to believe a church deacon with grandchildren could be behind the girl's disappearance. "It's probably just a similar license plate," she said. "Not the same one Abe Mast saw." That had been her fear all along. This whole thing was probably one big wild-goose chase.

"I guess we'll just have to see what we find," John said again.

Elizabeth asked about John's son, who was away at college, and his daughter, in high school, and soon they were pulling into the driveway of a tall wooden farmhouse painted a soft gray. A pristine white barn stood to the left, and inside Elizabeth could see half of an old-fashioned red tractor. The fields surrounding the yard were planted with corn. A blue Chevy pickup was parked in the driveway, next to a white Lincoln Continental. Elizabeth recognized the truck immediately. This was the truck she'd seen in the security footage.

"Here we are." John turned off the engine and stepped out, and Elizabeth pushed her door open. A big black dog came bounding out of the open barn door and ran toward them.

"Don't worry. He's friendly."

She looked up and saw a man with gray hair and denim coveralls over a white T-shirt waving at them from the barn door. Elizabeth recognized Walt right away. He was rounder, and his once-dark hair had faded, but it was him, no doubt about it. Walt tucked a rag into his back pocket and started walking toward them slowly, leaning on a four-footed cane.

The dog ran up to Elizabeth and sniffed her, and she held out her hand and let him lick it. "You must smell Pal," she said, patting the soft fur of his head.

"Batman, come here."

The dog bounded back over to Walt obediently. Elizabeth had to laugh. "Batman?"

Walt shook his head. "That's what happens when you let the grandkids name the dog." He shuffled toward them slowly, his face grim, and with each step, Elizabeth felt worse about this. Surely this nice elderly man could not be involved in this whole mess, and here they were disturbing him while he was working. "What can I do for you?"

John walked toward him in long strides, no doubt to save him the trouble of crossing the yard, and stopped in front of him. "I'm Officer John Marks." He held out his hand, and Walt shook it.

"And I'm Elizabeth Classen," she said, coming up beside John. "I believe you knew my father, Henry Classen."

"That's right." The taut look on Walt's face melted into a smile. "Well, look at that. It's been a while."

"Yes, it sure has." Elizabeth tried to keep her voice natural, as if this were just an ordinary conversation with an old friend. "I think the last time we saw each other was at my father's memorial service."

"That's right. It was a beautiful service."

"Thank you. We appreciated your coming."

"Of course, of course. And I was sorry to hear about your mother."

"Thank you." She was never sure how to respond to this, even more than six months after her mother had passed away. "It was a hard time, but I'm doing well. Both of my sisters moved home, and we reopened Secondhand Blessings."

"I'm glad to hear that," Walt said. "That must be some comfort."

"Yes, it is."

Elizabeth glanced over at John, who stepped forward again.

"We're sorry to interrupt you, but I was hoping I could ask you a few questions."

The confusion on Walt's face was genuine, Elizabeth was certain. But was there also...The way his eyes widened, and the lines on his forehead froze...It almost looked like he was nervous.

"Questions? About what?"

Well, fear was natural, she supposed. Most people were not used to being questioned by the police. Hopefully this would be over quickly, they could apologize, and he could get back to his tractors.

"About your whereabouts on Friday night."

"Friday night?" Walt ran a hand through his hair. "I was here. Watched the game on TV."

"Did you go out at all?"

There was a pause, just a fraction of a second too long. "No." Walt looked from John to Elizabeth and back again.

He was lying. They had seen his truck in the security camera footage, but even without knowing that, she would have been able to tell he was lying.

"Is there anyone else who might have borrowed your truck?"

He shifted, balancing his weight on his cane. "Why?"

"We're trying to find out about an incident that took place just before nine, over on Weavertown Road."

Another pause.

"What kind of incident?"

John cleared his throat, but didn't answer the question. "Did you see anything out of the ordinary Friday evening?"

"Just the Pirates mucking the game up. But that's not really all that unusual."

"Did you go out at all?" John asked again.

Again, a pause. Elizabeth heard her heart pounding in the silence that seemed to stretch on forever.

"Why?"

"We believe a girl was picked up from the side of the road. We're trying to find out what happened there, and we're wondering if you might have seen anything that would lead us to help identify her," John said. "Your truck was seen in the area, and it matches the description of the truck that we believe stopped for the girl."

His eyes darted around, and his breath seemed to be coming out in short, shallow gasps. For a moment, Elizabeth worried he was having a heart attack, or a stroke, or—

"All right," he said. "Okay, yes, I stopped for Annalise."

CHAPTER FOURTEEN

Mary was just settling down on the porch swing with a glass of lemonade when she heard her phone ring. Normally, she'd just let it ring—a lazy Sunday afternoon with a book was just what she needed—but Elizabeth was still out with John, and she was hoping for an update. Mary pushed herself up and hurried inside to grab her phone from where it was charging on the counter. She didn't recognize the number on the screen, but she answered anyway.

"Hello?" She carried the phone through the living room and back toward the front door.

"Hi, this is Kathleen Cooke, from the Lancaster Public Library."

"Oh. Hello." Mary hadn't expected to hear from her so soon. "Is the library open on Sundays?"

It was cooler on the covered porch than in the house, and a slight breeze stirred the air. She sat in the swing and let it rock back and forth.

"The library is not, but I was curious, so I did some digging on my own. And I found some information that might help your search."

"Really?" Mary had hoped she might find something, but she hadn't expected her to find anything so quickly. "What did you find?"

"It's kind of...complicated. I'd love to show you. When would be a good time?"

Mary glanced around the yard. Martha had taken Craig's family for a ride on the Strasburg Rail Road, and with Elizabeth gone, she was alone here. The store was closed on Sundays. Tomorrow she had to work in the shop, but today, she had no obligations.

"Would today work for you?" Mary asked.

"Actually, today would be great," Kathleen said. "Could you meet me at home?"

"That should be fine," Mary said. "What's the address?"

A few minutes later, Mary was in her car heading toward Lancaster. It wasn't hard to find the brick row house in the historic Chestnut Hill area of town. This part of town had many older homes and cute cafés and shops, and with the arching leafy trees and the old-fashioned narrow streets, it was quite charming. Mary had lived in a neighborhood not unlike it in Indianapolis with Brian before they'd had children. She parked in front of the house, which was situated in a stretch of red brick homes with arched windows and gingerbread trim on the covered porches. She loved the towering oak tree out front. Mary hadn't minded how close the houses were in neighborhoods like this when she was in her twenties and thirties, but after living on the farm, it was hard to imagine sharing a wall with a next-door neighbor again.

Mary picked up the sampler, which she'd wrapped in a towel and tucked into a shopping bag, and walked up to the front door and rang the doorbell. Kathleen pulled open the wooden door, which was painted a glossy black.

"Did you find it all right?" Kathleen was wearing knee-length shorts and a loose top, her hair pulled back into a messy knot. She stepped back and gestured for Mary to come in.

"No problems at all," Mary said. She stepped into the hallway and took in the pressed tin on the ceilings and the beautifully carved ornaments on the arched doorways. The woodwork maintained its original rich mahogany color, and the walls of the entry hall were painted a soft blue. The intricately carved staircase rose to the second floor, and she glimpsed a beautifully done living room that branched off to the right. "This is lovely."

"Thank you," Kathleen said. "I've always loved this stretch of houses, so when this place came up for sale, I convinced my husband we had to have it." She closed the door and gestured for Mary to follow her. "Our youngest had just left for college, and it seemed like a good time to downsize."

"It's got so much historic charm." If this was what downsizing meant to Kathleen, Mary couldn't imagine what her previous home must have been like. Kathleen gestured for Mary to follow her into a room off the main hallway, and they walked into a room covered in floor-to-ceiling bookshelves.

"You have your own library," Mary said, turning to take in the marble fireplace and the minimalist furniture that made up the seating area, but mostly the floor to ceiling books.

"This is what really sold me on this place," Kathleen said. "And I was able to convince my husband that I would be able to contain all my stuff in here instead of letting it creep all over the house." She laughed and gestured around the room. "As you can see, I'm still struggling with that."

Mary did see that there were books piled everywhere—not just on the shelves but on the coffee table and on the desk and on a side table.

"This is fantastic," Mary said. Though, given the chance, she'd choose a painting studio over her own personal library. But she would hardly turn up her nose at a room like this.

"I do enjoy books. But then, I guess that's fairly obvious." Kathleen laughed. "But my other passion is history, and I've had so much fun poking around in the records, trying to figure out what happened to your Frances."

Kathleen gestured for Mary to sit down on the blue velvet sofa, and she settled in next to her on a matching chair. Mary admired how the simple modern furniture gave the Victorian home a more contemporary feel. She set the bag with the sampler on the table in front of her.

"Is this it?" Kathleen asked.

"Yes. Here. Take a look." Mary pulled the sampler out of the bag and unwrapped the towel. She held it out, and Kathleen took it gently.

"Oh, wow." Kathleen looked down at the embroidered piece, taking in the hand-stitched alphabets, the Bible verse, the red-brick house. "This is exquisite in real life."

"I'm so glad you think so." She pointed to the period-spider stitched into the corner. "And look at that."

"Is that a spider?" Kathleen asked in amazement.

"It is." Mary smiled. "I like to imagine she added it at the very end, after her mother or school mistress or whoever approved of her work."

"I think that's a likely scenario," Kathleen said. "An interest in insects or spiders would hardly have been encouraged. This piece was meant to show off her skill with the needle, to advertise, in a way, her usefulness in running a household. Bugs were not exactly meant to be a part of that."

"I think that's why I like it so much," Mary said. "It shows her spirit." A piece of fluff from the towel had caught on the corner of the frame, and she brushed it aside.

"It does that," Kathleen said. "But it also does more. It actually gives us a clue about who she would eventually become."

"Really?" Mary looked up at Kathleen. "What did you find?"

"Well, the field of entomology was relatively new back then," Kathleen said.

"Entomology?"

"The study of insects."

Mary gave an involuntary shudder.

"I know, it sounds kind of awful, if you're imagining things like cockroaches. But it was an emerging field of study at the time, and bugs are actually quite fascinating if you can get past the ick factor."

"I don't think I could," Mary said.

"That's fair enough. It's not for me either," Kathleen said. "But I suspect the spider Frances embroidered here was an early clue about something she found interesting."

Mary cocked her head.

"Let me back up," Kathleen said. "First things first. You told me she was born in 1871 and married Clarence Matthews in 1891. And you discovered that Clarence had passed away in 1910. That was enough to get me started." Kathleen picked up a manila folder from the coffee table and opened it. "I did some research after you left the library yesterday, and then I was able to do some more from home here this morning. A lot of Lancaster County's historical records are online, which makes things very convenient."

Mary nodded, eager for her to go on.

"I discovered that Frances and Clarence bought a home in Lancaster, not far from here," Kathleen said.

"So she was upper class," Mary said.

"They would have been well off," Kathleen said. "This would have been about the same time the houses in this part of town were built, so it's likely they were the first owners. Well, I guess technically it would have been Clarence who was the first owner. Women couldn't own property back then."

It boggled Mary's mind to think about that. Women couldn't even vote until 1920.

"Do you know what Clarence did for a living?" Mary asked.

"I wasn't able to find that," Kathleen said. "But I think it's safe to assume they were comfortable."

Mary looked around Kathleen's home and tried to imagine it as it would have been when it was new. "There wouldn't have been electricity back then, would there?"

"No." Kathleen shook her head. "It would have been gas. When we renovated this place, we found the original gas pipes that would have powered the light fixtures and kitchen equipment."

"So they had lights, at least."

"Oh, yes. Probably very elaborate chandeliers and sconces. But they would have been dimmer than the incandescent lights we're used to." She gestured at the walls. "They probably would have had thick velvet curtains and flocked wallpaper and oriental carpets and lots of heavy furniture. The Victorian era was all about showing off your wealth."

"How long did they live here?" Mary asked.

"I didn't see a record of sale in the archives, so I'm guessing a long time. My guess is the house was passed down to one of their children after Clarence died. I'd have to locate a more recent bunch of records to find out exactly when it was sold."

"So they had children?"

"Oh, yes." Kathleen said again. "Four. One girl and three boys. Though one boy didn't make it to his first birthday."

"Oh dear." Mary couldn't imagine the sorrow Frances must have felt.

"I know. Of course that kind of thing was much more common back then, but that can't have made it any easier."

They were both quiet for a moment, then Kathleen continued. "The other three did live and grow into adulthood. I haven't found records for all of them yet, but it seems that the oldest boy married in 1915."

"That's good to hear," Mary said.

"I can continue to dig if you'd like," Kathleen said. "But I found something even more interesting."

"What's that?"

"Well, I thought about the spider Frances had embroidered on the sampler. As we've mentioned, it was unusual for a young girl to do something like that. And the name Matthews kept sticking in my mind. It took me a while to figure out why."

"What did you find?" Mary asked.

"My middle son was applying to college a few years back," Kathleen said.

Mary tilted her head. This wasn't going quite the way she had been expecting.

"He was interested in studying biology. We were pushing for Franklin and Marshall so he could live at home and save money."

Franklin and Marshall was a well-regarded private university in Lancaster, Mary knew.

"He ended up going to the University of Pennsylvania, but we spent some time touring the science buildings at Franklin and Marshall, and I remembered a small museum in the biology building." Kathleen's face had spread into a smile. "There was an especially interesting collection of insects, and I recalled reading that it had been donated by a private donor, a woman who had been fascinated with entomology."

"No." It couldn't be...

"So I called the college, and the nice student who answered the phone in the biology department did some digging for me. The director of the department called me back a while later, and confirmed that the start of the college's collection had been donated by a woman named Frances Matthews."

"You're serious?"

Kathleen nodded. "It seems that she was fascinated by bugs. Always had been. If she'd been born in another time, she might have gone on to be a leading entomologist. But given her circumstances, she was limited to collecting interesting specimens where she could find them. She managed to collect several hundred distinct types of insects in the area."

"Do you mean she had boxes of bugs in her house?" Mary was still trying to picture it.

"Not just hanging out in boxes, I don't think. I would imagine she preserved and mounted them."

"She stuck a pin through them and displayed them?" Mary had seen collections like this at museums, and they gave her the creeps.

"I suppose that's one way to say it." Kathleen shrugged. "It may not have been a hobby you or I would have chosen, but she managed to collect species that hadn't been studied around this area before. Apparently she advanced the study of entomology in the Lancaster area substantially. She was a scientist in her own way."

"That's incredible." Again, it wasn't a field Mary would have chosen for herself, but it was impressive nonetheless.

"There aren't a lot of records, but the director of the department told me they had some old journals and collection notes that you could review if you were interested."

"I might try to check them out sometime." She looked back down at the sampler, and especially at the spider Frances had stitched in the corner. To think that this little girl had grown up, gotten married, and had children—all the things well-bred ladies were supposed to do in that time. But she'd also managed to study something that interested her, despite the time she'd grown up in, and advanced the science of the field. It was amazing, really.

"It's funny, isn't it?" Kathleen mused. "How stories like Frances's would just be forgotten if no one bothered to ask about them?"

"It is," Mary agreed. "Maybe that's why the things we leave behind are so important." She looked down at the sampler again. It was such a simple thing, really. Hardly special in its time. Every well-bred young lady made something similar. But it had caught her eye because hidden in all the beautiful embroidery and flowers and well-chosen Bible verses, Frances had left a tiny little piece of who she really was. That little bit of authenticity among the expected was what had attracted Mary, had made this piece stand out. Mary hoped that kind of authenticity came through in her paintings, and in all she did, really. If Mary's artistic work was to be of any value to the world, it needed to reflect who she was. She prayed the Lord would allow her work to reflect His glory.

"There's one more thing I found," Kathleen said, flipping through the papers in her folder.

"What's that?" Mary looked at what Kathleen held out. It took her a minute to make out what Kathleen was showing her, but when it registered, it hit her like a physical punch.

"Oh my."

Kathleen shook the paper. "Take a look."

CHAPTER FIFTEEN

Elizabeth couldn't have heard that right. "What did you say?"

"I picked her up," Walt said. "The girl by the side of the road? Friday night? That's who you're asking about, right?"

Elizabeth couldn't believe it. Had he really just admitted to what she thought he had? And he'd given them a name—Annalise.

"That's right." John managed to recover himself faster than Elizabeth. "So you *did* pick her up?"

Walt sniffed, and he nodded toward the house. "Let's go inside where it's cool."

It felt like it took a lifetime for Walt to shuffle across the yard. John helped him up the steps, and they walked through a small mudroom into the kitchen of the old farmhouse. The counters were a yellow vinyl, and the cabinets were of solid oak that had darkened over the years. The linoleum floor was worn to white in patches. John focused on helping Walt get to the kitchen safely.

"Have a seat," Walt said, gesturing toward the table in the middle of the room. Elizabeth lowered herself into one of the metal and vinyl chairs, and John sat across from her.

"Can I get you anything to drink?" Walt asked.

"Water would be great, thank you," John said. Walt looked at Elizabeth, and she nodded.

Walt moved to the counter and filled two glasses from the filtration pitcher on the counter. Elizabeth hopped up and carried the glasses to the table for him, and he hobbled to the table. Then Walt slowly lowered himself into a chair.

Elizabeth thanked Walt and took a sip. The filtration system couldn't quite remove the tang of sulfur.

"Can you tell us what happened Friday night?" John asked, his voice so much calmer than Elizabeth was capable of making hers at this point.

"I was out of milk, and I knew I'd want some for coffee in the morning," Walt said. "June used to always take care of things like that, and I never seem to notice until the last minute when I'm out of something. Well, anyway, it was late, but I knew I'd want milk, so I got in the truck and went out. The Pirates were down by four runs, so I figured it wouldn't hurt to leave at that point anyway."

Elizabeth wanted him to stop talking about inconsequential things and get to the point—what he had done with the girl from the side of the road—but something in her said he wouldn't be rushed. Besides, it was really John's place to lead this investigation. She tried to be patient.

Walt leaned back in the chair, adjusting the cane at his side, and the chair squeaked beneath him.

"Used to be I'd just go out to the tank and help myself to some milk, but we stopped keeping cows over a decade ago."

"That must have been a big change," Elizabeth said gently, practicing the patience she knew she needed. Even just a few cows were a huge amount of work, and she'd seen farmers who couldn't keep up with it as they aged. "Do you still plant the fields?"

"I rent it all out now," Walt said. "None of my kids wanted to take the place over. Can't say's I blame them, really. It's a tough life."

"That it is," Elizabeth said. "My parents never went on a real vacation. A lot of people don't realize how hard farmers work." It seemed to please him, and he nodded.

"So you went out to get milk on Friday night," John said, bringing them back to the topic at hand. "And then what happened?"

"I was driving down Weavertown Road, out by that place where there's that bridge over the culvert. I saw a light by the side of the road."

"Can you describe the light?"

"It was white. Like, you know, light."

Walt looked at John like he was nuts, so Elizabeth clarified. "Could you tell where it was coming from?"

"I assumed it was a flashlight but one of those small ones. Not one that would give you enough light to really see what's out there on a country road at night. It was bouncing up and down like someone was walking. I thought that was strange. You don't see too many people walking by the side of the road 'round these parts, especially at night. It's not safe."

"What did you do?" John asked.

"I slowed down and pulled over." Again, John gave Elizabeth a look that said John was clueless. Elizabeth put a smile on her face and gestured for Walt to continue talking. "I figured whoever it was needed help. Why else would you be out there like that?"

"And what did you find when you pulled over?" Elizabeth asked.

"It was a girl," Walt said. He used his thumbnail to scratch at some dried food stuck to the surface of the table. "The side of the road is no place for a teenage girl at night, so I stopped and asked her if she needed a ride."

"Did you recognize the girl?" John asked.

"Not at first."

He didn't elaborate, and Elizabeth fought the urge to ask more. John seemed content to let the silence stretch out.

"I know her dad," Walt finally said. "I'd never met her, but I realized who her dad was pretty quick."

"How do you know her father?" John asked.

Another pause.

"He owns a farm not too far from here. We run into each other from time to time."

John seemed to be trying to figure out what to make of that answer.

"What did she say when you asked her about the ride?" John asked.

"She said thanks, and she hopped into the truck."

Elizabeth had so many questions. How would the phone, left behind, have been set to blink an SOS if Walt's intentions had been as innocent as he was making them seem?

"So she came into the truck willingly?" she asked.

"Of course." Now Walt gave her the same withering look he'd given John. "What do you think?"

Elizabeth backtracked quickly. "Oh, of course, I didn't mean—obviously you wouldn't have done anything..." She looked at John, hoping for rescue.

"We're just trying to understand the sequence of events," John said, his voice calm. "So she said she'd be glad to take a ride?"

"Yes," he said, very slowly and deliberately. "I asked if she needed a ride, and she said thanks, she'd sure appreciate it. Then she got into the truck."

"And then what happened?" John asked.

Walt looked from John to Elizabeth and back again.

"What's this all about?" he asked. Elizabeth studied him. There was something he wasn't saying.

"We're trying to find her," John said.

It was true, even if it wasn't the whole truth, Elizabeth thought.

"Why?" Even if the look on his face hadn't shown he was hiding something, the hitch in his voice would have given it away.

"We found her phone by the side of the road, right where you picked her up," John said evenly. He'd seen Walt's reaction too.

"She dropped her phone?" Walt asked.

"That's right," John said. "And we're trying to find her." John was watching Walt carefully, trying to read his features as he spoke. "Did she have her phone when she got into the truck?"

"I assumed so, but honestly I couldn't say." Walt said. "I wasn't really paying attention to her phone. I was trying to figure out where she was going and whether she was okay. There are all kinds of reasons a girl could be walking alone by the side of the road, and most of them aren't good."

"What did she say?" But even as John asked the question, Elizabeth already knew the answer.

"Her car broke down," Walt said. "She was walking home."

The car that Martha had found abandoned at the side of the road. They'd been right about this, at least.

"So I offered her a ride," he said, repeating the words slowly and loudly, as if John were hard of hearing. "And she got into the truck."

"How old is Annalise?" John asked.

"I don't know. Teenager. Somewhere in there." He shrugged. "I didn't ask."

"Did you notice anything out of the ordinary as you drove away?" Elizabeth asked. She knew she should let John ask the questions, but she couldn't help herself. Surely one of them would have noticed a blinking strobe light at the side of the road.

"I can't say I did. I was listening to the game on the radio, and the Pirates got a grand slam. I wanted to get home to see the rest of the game on TV."

Elizabeth glanced at John, but he was focused on Walt.

"Where did you drop her off?"

"At her house." Again, a look that she couldn't read.

"Where is that?" John asked.

Walt waited just a beat too long before he answered. "A farm, over on Paradise Road, right by Cherry Hill Road." He took a sip, then continued. "Used to be the Mazeroski place, years ago."

Elizabeth couldn't picture the place, but John nodded as he wrote the information down.

"What happened when you drove up?" John asked.

"Well, I pulled into the driveway and slowed down," Walt said, with exaggerated slowness. "And then I stopped the truck.

She got out, said thanks, and went inside. I turned around and headed home."

"Were there any lights on in the house? Or cars in the driveway?"

"Can't say I noticed," Walt said. "It was the bottom of the eighth. I'd done a good deed, and I wanted to get home. Had no idea giving a young girl a ride on a country road was a capital offense."

He was annoyed at the questions, and if Elizabeth was honest, she understood. It sounded like a nice man had done a girl a favor, and she had simply lost her phone in the process. Elizabeth could understand why he was frustrated about being questioned by the police for doing a good deed. Then again, he'd lied to them when they first got here, and she was almost certain he was hiding something now. Was the incident as innocent as he was making it out to be?

"Is there anything else you can tell us about Friday night?" John asked.

Walt shook his head. "That's the long and short of it. I saw someone who needed help, I gave her help, and I drove home. Made it home in time for the ninth inning."

"Polanco made a great catch, didn't he?" John asked. "Kept the Mets from scoring again."

Walt paused a moment and swallowed before nodding. "Sure did."

There was an awkward pause. Something was communicated between the men in the silence that Elizabeth didn't understand. But then John stood and held out his hand.

"You'll let us know if you remember anything more about what happened Friday night?" he asked.

"Of course."

Elizabeth thanked Walt for his help, and then they walked back out to the police cruiser.

"I guess that solves that," Elizabeth said as she climbed into the passenger seat. "Shall we head on out to Paradise and return Annalise's phone?"

John didn't say anything for a moment. He buckled himself into the car and put the key in the ignition. Elizabeth felt the need to fill the silence that stretched out, but restrained herself.

"I don't know," John said, turning the key. The engine roared to life. "I'm not sure it's that simple." He put the car in reverse and turned it around.

"You don't believe him," Elizabeth said to fill the awkward silence.

"I'm not sure," John said. He looked at Elizabeth.

"He was hiding something," Elizabeth said. "I mean, sure, he lied to us at first, but after that, there was something he wasn't telling us."

"Why did he lie when we first got there? That's my first question," John said.

"Maybe he was nervous," Elizabeth said. "I'm sure a lot of people must be nervous when the police show up and start asking questions."

John didn't answer right away, and for a moment the low hum of the engine was the only sound.

She tried again. "Why are you quiet like that?"

"I'm trying to decide whether to take you back home before I go check out the address he gave us," John finally admitted.

Elizabeth turned her head. "What? Why?"

"I'm not sure what we'll find there, and the last thing I'd want to do is put you in any danger."

"What do you mean?"

"I'm trying to picture that area in my mind. Do you remember seeing a farm there?"

Elizabeth thought, then she shook her head. "But I don't know every property in the area."

"Neither do I. But even if there is a farm there, he said something else strange."

Elizabeth sat quietly and waited for him to go on.

"He told us the house where he dropped Annalise off was the old Mazeroski place. Mazeroski was a second baseman for the Pirates when I was a kid. He famously hit a homerun in the bottom of the ninth inning of the seventh game of the World Series to win it all for Pittsburgh."

"Maybe it's a coincidence. They have the same name."

"Maybe," John said, but the tone of his voice made it clear he didn't think so.

"He's a Pirates fan. You think he made up the name of the people who owned the farm," Elizabeth said.

"I think it's an extraordinary coincidence, if not," John said.

John hesitated a moment longer, and then he sighed and lifted his foot off the brake and pulled out onto the road. He hadn't turned toward the Classen farm, so she knew he'd decided to let her come along.

"Why would he lie?" Elizabeth asked the question again.

"That's what I want to find out," John said, as the car hummed beneath them. "I think he was telling us the truth at first. I believe he did stop and pick up the girl, and probably with good motivations."

"It's hard to imagine Walt intending to kidnap her," Elizabeth said. "It would be the slowest kidnapping in history."

John laughed. "I agree with you there. I think that after the initial lie, he mostly told us the truth for a while. But then he shifted at some point, and I'm trying to figure out why that is."

Elizabeth considered this. There had been a couple of things in the conversation that hadn't completely added up for her.

"Do you really think he didn't notice the phone's strobe light when she dropped it?"

"It seems hard to believe that neither of them noticed it," John said. "But the only other option is that he made her leave her phone behind, and why would he do that?"

"I don't know." None of the options that ran through her mind were good. "But why would he do a good deed and then lie about it to the police?"

John shrugged. "People often react strangely to being questioned by the police." He flipped on his blinker and slowed at the corner of Paradise Road. "Innocent people admit to crimes they didn't do, and guilty people get scared and say whatever it takes to cover up their crimes. You never know."

"But it wasn't like you dragged him into an interrogation room and tortured him. We were in his home and asking him pleasant questions."

"You'd be surprised what seeing a police car drive up can do to people sometimes," John said. "I'm not saying it made Walt nervous, but it can do that to some people."

Elizabeth wondered if he'd driven the squad car today on purpose, to have that effect, but decided not to ask.

"So which parts do you think he's lying about?"

"I'm not sure," John said. "But we should be coming to that farm where he said he dropped her off very soon." John slowed as they approached the intersection where Paradise Road met Cherry Hill Road. There was an old white church on one corner, and cornfields on the others. There were no farms, no houses of any kind within a quarter mile of the intersection.

"Why would he lie about where he dropped her off?" Elizabeth asked.

"I don't know," John said. Something in his voice made it very clear that he wasn't pleased.

CHAPTER SIXTEEN

The afternoon sun beat down, and there was very little shade in the yard, but that didn't deter Dylan. The kid had more energy than the Energizer Bunny.

"Come on, Grandma," he said, pulling on her arm.

"All right. Go get your shoes on." Martha gestured toward the front door, where the family's shoes lay in a pile. Dylan ran down the hallway, skidding on the rag rug at the bottom of the stairs and riding it like a surfboard.

"Kevin?" Martha stood in the doorway of the living room and looked in at where her older grandson was—predictably—absorbed in something on his phone. "We're going out to see the goats. Do you want to come?"

"No, thanks."

She supposed he'd at least shown good manners, but somehow it didn't make her feel any better.

She tried again. "Are you sure?"

"I'm sure." He didn't look up.

Martha hovered in the doorway, trying to decide what to do. Part of her knew that he was a kid, and this was his vacation, and he would come up for air when he got tired of staring at that silly screen. But another part of her couldn't help being hurt that he would rather talk to his friends on his phone than spend time with her. She never got to see him anymore, and while she was hardly infirm, it wasn't like she was going to be around forever. Besides, she'd read the articles about how screen time was changing kids' brains. About how this generation was more depressed and disconnected than any in history because they spent so much time on virtual friendships and so little time on actual personal interactions.

"Kevin." She used her mom voice, and he did at least look up at the sound. "You don't have to come out to see the animals, but please put your phone down and spend some time in the real world."

At first he just wrinkled his brow, and for a moment she almost thought he was going to listen. But then he rolled his eyes and said, "I don't want to go out and see the stupid goats. It's hot, and they're stinky."

It felt almost as if he'd slapped her. Martha tried her best not to show how the words made her feel. She took in a long, deep breath.

"You don't have to see the goats," she said. "I'm just asking you to put the phone away and spend some of this trip paying attention to people around you, not the people inside your phone."

"There are no people inside the phone," he said. "They're my friends, and they're just as real as everyone else."

"Uh-oh...," Dylan said from behind her. "Wrong thing to say."

Martha decided to ignore Dylan's commentary. She took in another deep breath. Martha had raised three children, and this was hardly the first time she'd gotten sass from one of her progeny. The circumstances may be new—she hadn't had to worry about cell phones when her kids were young—but the challenges of raising respectful children were not. Martha had faced this before, and she knew what to do.

Please Lord, let me say this right, she prayed.

"Kevin?"

He looked up at her.

"Put the phone away."

He opened his mouth to argue, but he must have seen something in her face or heard something in her tone of voice that made him reconsider. He froze, stared at her, his eyes wide. And then, slowly, reluctantly, he tucked the phone into his pocket. She couldn't read the look on his face, but it was clear that he wasn't happy. Still, he'd obeyed.

Martha should have felt triumphant, but all she felt was sad.

When John dropped Elizabeth back off at home, she invited him inside for some pie and coffee, but he said he had to get back to the station and talk to his team about what he'd discovered. Elizabeth felt a bit disappointed, but she understood, and she thanked him for a fun afternoon before she headed into the house.

A fun afternoon? She could have kicked herself as soon as the words were out of her mouth. John was working on a potential kidnapping case, and here she was acting as if he'd taken her to the fair. Good grief.

Elizabeth closed the door behind her, and she saw that Martha was in the kitchen.

"Hi there," Elizabeth said, setting her purse by the door. "How's it going in here?"

"Okay," Martha said. "Craig and Molly are taking naps, and the kids are in their room. So I figured I'd get started on dinner this evening. I'm making lasagna. It's Dylan's favorite."

The way Martha was grating that cheese, as if she had a vendetta against it, made Elizabeth wary.

"Is everything okay?"

"It's fine." Her tone indicated that it was not, in fact, fine, but that she didn't want to talk about it.

"You know, you don't have to handle all the cooking and baking, even when your family is here," Elizabeth said carefully.

"I know," Martha said. "But I enjoy it."

If she grated cheese that way because she enjoyed it, Elizabeth would hate to see her when she was upset.

Truthfully, Elizabeth suspected it was more than enjoyment that motivated her. Martha wasn't very good at expressing her feelings in words. Cooking for people was how she showed her love, Elizabeth knew. Best to just leave her to it.

Elizabeth grabbed her laptop and plopped down on one of the kitchen chairs.

"How was your afternoon? Was that John dropping you off?" Martha finished grating the cheese and brushed her hands together.

Elizabeth told her about the visit to Walt Goodwin's house, and Martha seemed as shocked as Elizabeth had been by the lies he'd told.

"Why would he lie?" Martha asked.

"He's obviously hiding something," Elizabeth said. "And I'm going to find out what it is."

Martha looked dubious. "You're going to find out what he's lying about by looking at your computer?"

"Do you have any better ideas?"

Martha opened a jar of homemade marinara sauce and poured some into the baking dish, and then she said, "I'd start with trying to find out if the girl's name was really Annalise."

"And how would you go about doing that?" Elizabeth asked.

Martha used a rubber spatula to spread the sauce out. "Walt told you she was a teenager?"

Elizabeth nodded. Where was Martha going with this?

"And she wasn't Amish, right?"

"No, I don't think so. He'd have mentioned that."

"Then I'd probably try to find out if there's a girl named Annalise at the local high school, for starters. You might be able to find a last name, if there is."

That *was* a good idea. "But how? It's Sunday. And it's July. We can't call the school."

Martha used tongs to lift a cooked noodle from a pot on the stove and let the water drip off it. "I guess the first place I'd look would be a yearbook, if there was one available."

Martha was just full of good ideas today. There had to be a way to get her hands on a high school yearbook. John's daughter, Tina, might have one, but Elizabeth didn't think she could get in touch with Tina without alerting John to what she was doing. She thought for a moment, and then realized the

Gallegos family down the road had kids in high school. Elizabeth pushed herself up and flipped through Mama's little Rolodex by the phone to find their number. Cynthia Gallegos answered the phone on the first ring, and if she was surprised by Elizabeth's request, she didn't show it.

"Of course," Cynthia said. "Marisol has this year's yearbook. She's been paging through it every day, moaning about how she misses her friends. You'd make my life easier if you borrowed it for a while."

"I guess I'll run over to the Gallegos house," Elizabeth said when she hung up the phone. She didn't know the family well, but they were always warm and kind, and every Christmas Eve they brought over a plate of amazing homemade tamales. She hopped in her car and drove the half mile to their home, a neat two-story surrounded by trees and a sloping lawn. Daddy had always been jealous of the riding mower Anthony used to keep the grass neat, Elizabeth remembered. Inside the house, the TV was on, and there was music blaring from one of the upstairs bedrooms. Elizabeth smiled to think that even if she hadn't known teenagers lived here, she'd have figured it out. She chatted with Cynthia for a few moments, and then Cynthia handed her the most recent high school yearbook. It was a thick, heavy book with a glossy red cover bearing the logo of Conestoga Valley High School.

"I promised Marisol you'd return it tomorrow," Cynthia said. "She was very concerned she'd never see it again, and then how would she mope around in her room missing her friends?"

"I will take good care of it," Elizabeth promised. "Thank you so much."

Cynthia hadn't even asked why Elizabeth wanted to borrow it, she realized as she drove back home. She appreciated Marisol's sharing one of her most treasured possessions, even if she hadn't shared it willingly.

Martha had set the lasagna in the oven by the time Elizabeth got home. Someone was moving around upstairs, but otherwise the house was quiet.

"Did you get it?" Martha was rinsing a bowl in the sink.

"I did." Elizabeth set the yearbook down on the table and sat down in her chair. She flipped open the cover and saw that every square inch of the first few pages had been covered in messages from Marisol's friends. *Have a great summer. Don't ever change. Don't do anything I wouldn't do.* It was pretty much the same stuff Elizabeth had written to her own friends in high school.

"If she was driving a car, she'd probably be a junior or a senior," Martha said. Elizabeth nodded and flipped to the second half of the book. She started with the last names that started with *A*, looking for an Annalise among the senior class. These kids looked like babies, Elizabeth thought. How could they be seniors in high school? She saw a few faces she recognized from church and the neighborhood, but there was no Annalise mentioned.

"She wasn't a senior," Elizabeth reported. Martha nodded from where she was tossing a salad. Elizabeth started with the junior class, looking at each name. She was almost ready to give up when, in the *W* section, she saw something.

"Waters," she said. The picture showed a pretty girl with shoulder-length brown hair and straight white teeth. She looked like she belonged in an ad for toothpaste or shampoo. "Annalise Waters."

"What?" Martha came over to study the picture.

"There's an Annalise Waters. She was a junior last year."

"That has to be her."

Elizabeth had already flipped to the back of the book, where each student's name was listed in an index. Annalise was apparently featured in half a dozen places throughout the book, and Elizabeth flipped to the indicated pages and found that she had been in the 4-H club and the school play and the spring musical, as well as playing on the basketball team. Judging by the photos on the musical page, she had been the star of this year's production of *Guys and Dolls*.

"Do you know a Waters family around here?" Martha asked.

Elizabeth thought for a moment and shook her head. "No. But then, I don't know everyone." She had lived here long enough to know most of the old-timers, but there were so many families moving into the area these days.

"It seems that Walt was telling the truth about her name, at any rate," Elizabeth continued. "But we still don't know why he lied about where he dropped her off."

"I guess the next step is to find out where she really lives," Martha said. "And to see if you can track her down."

Elizabeth had been thinking the same thing. She walked to the shelf by the phone, where the phone book always sat. She flipped through the white pages, but there was no listing for a Waters.

"She was driving a car registered to Jack DiNapoli," Martha said. "See if there's a DiNapoli family listed in there."

Elizabeth scanned the *D* names, but there wasn't an entry for DiNapoli.

"Try Google," Martha said. "You can find everything on the internet these days."

Elizabeth pulled out her laptop and ran a search for "Waters Lancaster" but most of the results that came up had to do with local rivers and information about plumbing in the local Amish homes. She'd already tried a search for "DiNapoli Lancaster," but she tried it again now, and that, too, came up empty.

Next, she did a search for Annalise Waters, and she found a few social media sites, but they were locked, available only to her friends. Strong privacy settings made good sense, Elizabeth thought, but they were frustrating now.

How else could she find out where Annalise lived?

"If she was in 4-H, she probably lived on a farm," she thought out loud.

"That's likely." Martha was sprinkling cheese over the dish. "But that hardly narrows it down."

"True." Elizabeth tried to think. "Maybe we could ask some of her friends where she lives or how to get in touch with her."

"How would we do that?"

Elizabeth flipped to the pages of the yearbook that showed the production of *Guys and Dolls.* "If she's this involved with theater, she's got theater friends," she said.

"True," Martha said. "I suppose if we could get in touch with some of them..."

But Elizabeth was already looking up the name Rory Adler online. Rory had played the role of Nathan Detroit in *Guys and Dolls*, judging by the photo. She turned to the phone book and searched for the name Adler, but there were four listed in the area. Short of calling each of them—which she would do if needed—she wasn't sure how to find out which was Rory's family. It wasn't hard to find Rory's social media, but his posts were locked. Pictured next to Rory was Melissa Hansen, who had played Miss Adelaide. Melissa had red hair and big blue eyes, and she had an Instagram feed that documented what seemed like every moment of her life.

"Is that...?"

Elizabeth jumped. "Goodness." When had Martha come up behind her? "You shouldn't sneak up on people like that."

"I didn't sneak. You were just too absorbed to notice. Scroll back up."

"What?"

"I thought I saw something."

Elizabeth scrolled up, toward the pictures at the top of the feed.

"Stop," Martha said. These were posts from a few months back. "Look at that." She pointed to an image on the screen that showed a group of teens huddled around a baby goat. The goat was black and white and tiny and had to be only days old, and it looked terrified, but the kids looked thrilled. Melissa was in the center, holding the goat, and three other teen girls were around her.

"See there?"

Elizabeth squinted, and then she saw what Martha had seen. To the left of Melissa, two girls made that weird duck face that all the kids seemed to use in pictures these days. And there, on the right, was Annalise.

"So they were definitely friends."

"But look where they are."

Elizabeth looked at the picture again, and she sucked in a breath. Could it really have been this easy?

CHAPTER SEVENTEEN

Mary looked down at the picture of the red-brick house in the sampler, and then up at it in real life. This was it. This had to be it. The real house was tucked away on what was probably once a quiet country lane, but now was surrounded by newer houses and, at the corner, a restaurant and several small shops. Elm and spruce and plane trees arched overhead, dappling the sunlight and shading the home. The house was set right on the road, as older homes often were, and had white shutters and a black door. The door in the sampler had been green, and there was an Audi parked in the gravel driveway next to the home, but otherwise, little appeared to have changed.

This was the house Frances had grown up in, the one she'd stitched onto the sampler she'd made when she was twelve. Kathleen had found the address in the archives, and Mary was strangely pleased to see it, to know that it was still standing. That this piece of Frances's history still stood.

For a moment, Mary considered going to the door and asking the current owners to see the inside, but she knew how nuts she would sound, asking to tour the home of someone she had no real connection to who'd lived here a hundred and fifty years previously. In any case, it wasn't the inside that really interested her. The facade, depicted in such careful stitches, was what she'd come here to see.

She turned and headed toward her ultimate destination, which was just a few miles down the road. She found the cemetery easily enough, surrounded by a pretty rock wall and guarded by an iron gate. Kathleen had located a burial record for Frances, and Mary had come here to see it for herself. She pulled into the small parking lot and made her way down the meandering paths toward what looked like the oldest section of headstones. Flowers and small flags adorned many of the newer gravesites, but the quiet older section was largely undisturbed.

Some of the headstones from this section dated back to the 1700s. Mary couldn't even imagine it. Her ancestors had still been in Switzerland at that point, and this area would have been mostly woods, she guessed. She wandered, looking at the headstones, smiling at some of the old-fashioned names. Ebenezer, and Prudence, and Enoch, and Abraham. Well, actually, that one was still common among the Amish in the area. Some of the headstones were simple slabs, while others were more ornate, and some of the engraving was so worn she could barely make out the names. Finally, though, she found it, tucked away in a quiet corner. The headstone was a plain white rectangle, and the words carved into it were lined with moss, but there it was, next to the headstone that marked Clarence's grave.

Here lies Frances Matthews
Beloved wife, mother, and daughter
February 9, 1871–March 23, 1937
May she rest in her eternal reward

Tears started to sting Mary's eyes, and she fought them back. She knew it was silly. Of course Frances had passed away.

She would have been close to one hundred and fifty years old by now. Mary had never thought she was still around some-where—this was where they would all end up, she knew. Or where their bodies would end up, in any case. Mary had faith that there was more than this life, that she would one day see her Savior face-to-face and be reunited with her beloved mama and daddy, and with all who had gone before her. Maybe she'd even get to meet Frances.

But still, for some reason, it made her sad to see this grave-stone here and now. To see the final resting place of the woman she had grown to care more about than she had realized. Mary felt like she knew Frances in some small way, and seeing this here, now, well...She knew Martha would laugh to hear her say it, but it almost felt like losing a friend.

Mary reached out and put her hand on the stone, cool even in the heat of the summer day. "Thank you," she said, though she wasn't even sure exactly what she was thanking Frances for. For being who God had made her to be, even in a society that didn't support it, she supposed. For pursuing her passions in a world that hadn't wanted her to. For advancing the cause of science in her own way, even if it was the science of creepy crawly bugs.

Mary stood and studied the headstone for a few more min-utes. She'd found her, and for some reason, that felt import-ant. And then, reluctantly, she turned to go.

The phone rang and rang, and John wasn't picking up. Why wasn't he answering? They had figured out Annalise's last name and where she lived, and Elizabeth wanted to tell him right away. She left a voice mail for him, and then she turned back to Martha. "So what do we do now?"

Martha came around from behind her and lowered herself into the chair next to her. The sink was full of dishes, and the cheese was still sitting out on the counter. If Martha was leaving all that and coming to sit with her, she was really interested in figuring this out.

"I suppose now that we know where she lives, we should go there and see what we find," Martha said. "Maybe she's fine and just confused about what happened to her phone."

Elizabeth admired her sister's optimism. She turned back to the image they'd found on the screen. Most of the shot was taken up by the three girls cuddling a baby goat, but Martha had noticed something interesting in the background. At the top left edge of the screen, she could just make out the top third of a grain silo. Elizabeth wasn't sure how Martha had noticed it, but once she pointed it out, Elizabeth recognized it immediately. The silo was a familiar sight. Most of the grain silos in these parts were a dingy white or gray, but this silo sat up on a rise and had been painted with a beautifully rendered waving American flag, and underneath that, the words One Nation under God. Every time Elizabeth saw it, she said a little prayer of thanks to live in this country, and that, despite the differences that sometimes divided people, God was still watching over them all. She didn't know who had painted the silo, but she knew exactly where it was, just a few miles away on a back road. But the most interesting part of the image was the text that Melissa had written next to the image. *Adorable baby goats at Annalise's place. It's almost enough to make me want to live on a farm...almost.* If this picture had been taken at Annalise's home, then the memorable silo was either on her family's property or nearby.

"If we don't find anything there, then we should probably talk to her friends. If we want to find out where Annalise is and why she left her phone behind, we ask her friends what they know."

It seemed so logical when Martha said it. So obvious.

But it wasn't that simple.

"Are we allowed to talk to minors like that?"

"What do you mean? Of course we are," Martha said. "We're not the police. What's to stop us from tracking down Melissa Hansen or Rory Adler to ask if they know where Annalise is?"

Elizabeth saw that Martha was right, of course. But it didn't seem appropriate, somehow. And more than that, she wasn't sure if that was the best course of action. She put her head down into her hands to think.

"This whole time, we've been thinking the girl who dropped her phone was kidnapped," Elizabeth said. "A repeat of the Amber Barber case from so many years ago."

"That's what it sounded like, given the story we heard from Abe Mast, and also the fact that the phone was set to blink SOS and left behind."

"And the fact that someone named Viv has texted Annalise repeatedly, asking where she is and if something has happened to her. Viv was expecting her somewhere, and she didn't show up."

"And we have no idea if the reason she didn't show up was because she was kidnapped, she changed her mind about going wherever it was, or if she couldn't make it because her car broke down," Martha said.

Elizabeth snapped her fingers. "I know—we should look for a Viv in the yearbook. What if this is one of her friends, and she was headed to her house?"

"Now you're thinking straight," said Martha. She went to a drawer and pulled out a storage bag for the cheese.

Elizabeth spent the next ten minutes carefully looking for a Viv in the students' photographs. She finally closed the book with a heavy sigh. "Nothing. Whoever Viv is, they didn't go to school at Conestoga last year."

"So we still have the same questions," Martha said.

"Right," Elizabeth said. "What happened to Annalise? Why did she set her phone to blink SOS? Why hasn't she tried to find it? What happened to the car by the side of the road? Was she driving it? If so, how is she connected to Jack DiNapoli, who the car was registered to?"

"And how is either Jack or Annalise connected to whoever left that receipt from our store in the front seat?" Martha added.

"We don't even know for sure the phone really belongs to Annalise. We only have Walt Goodwin's word that this is the girl he picked up on the side of the road. Since we know he was lying about part of what he said, how do we know this for sure?"

They were both quiet for a minute, thinking. Elizabeth's mind was going in circles. It seemed that the more they learned, the more confused she got.

"We need to unlock the phone," Martha said. "I can't help but think that if we could just get into that phone, we'd be able to answer many of these questions."

Elizabeth had to agree. She knew how much of their lives young people today recorded on their phones. They would be able to find out more about who Viv was and whether there were emails or texts on the phone that laid out previous plans. They would be able to see pictures and her contacts and, hopefully, where she was now.

"So, again, what do we do now?" Elizabeth asked.

"I think there are two things we need to do." Martha held up one finger. "We should look into Walt Goodwin and try to understand why he lied and what the truth really is. And"—a second finger came up—"we need to go here." She used her other hand to point to the silo in the picture that was still on the screen.

Though she knew it sometimes drove Mary crazy, Elizabeth was more thankful than ever for Martha's logical mind.

"Good thinking." Elizabeth looked up at the round clock over the kitchen sink. It was faded and had never been nice to begin with, but it had been there for decades, and it brought Elizabeth great comfort. "I guess I'll go now to check out the farm. Will you have time to do some research on Walt before the kids come downstairs?"

"No." Martha crossed her arms over her chest. "I will not."

Elizabeth wasn't sure what to say. Martha no doubt had a long list of tasks she had been planning to accomplish this evening, but it wasn't like her to speak in that tone of voice.

"I won't, because I'm coming with you to the farm."

Elizabeth felt a smile spread across her face. "Wait. Really?"

"Sure. Why not?"

"You have a lasagna in the oven, for one thing. And Craig and Molly will be downstairs soon."

"I'll set a timer and leave a note asking them to take the lasagna out when it goes off. And it won't kill them to have a few minutes here without me."

"There are dirty dishes in the sink."

Martha pushed herself up. "They'll wait. Let's go find this missing girl."

"I think it's right up there," Martha said as she looked from her phone's screen to the windshield and back. The silo with the American flag was just up ahead, and they were trying to find the approximate spot the photo had been taken so they could figure out where exactly Annalise's home was. "I think we need to turn right at the corner, and then we should find the spot where the goat pen is."

"Got it." Elizabeth slowed and turned right at the stop sign, and then she drove along the road slowly until they came to a driveway. At the end of the driveway was a blue farmhouse and a red barn and white silo at the edge of the yard. There was a heavy-equipment trailer parked next to several outbuildings, including what looked like a tractor shed to the left of the barn, and to the right of the barn was a penned-in area that looked like it could be the spot where the photo with the goats had been taken in April. There were no cars in the driveway, and an odd stillness hung over the whole place.

"This has to be it." They could just see the top of the flag silo from here, and Martha was almost certain that from the pen by the barn they would see it at the same angle that had been captured in the photograph. They climbed out of the car and walked to the pen just to be sure, and when Martha held the image on her phone up, they saw that this was indeed the spot where it had been taken.

"This is it," Elizabeth confirmed. "This must be where Annalise lives."

Martha agreed. In the still evening, she could hear noises from inside the barn—animals moving, shuffling, nickering. But the yard was still, and there was no movement from inside the house.

"Let's go see if anyone's home," Martha said, but even as the words came out of her mouth, she knew what the answer would be. Still, she led her sister across the yard and around to the front of the house. There was a side door that led directly to the driveway, but they headed toward the front entrance. They walked up the narrow concrete porch slab and rang the doorbell, listening as it echoed inside the house. There was no sound, no movement at all. There were no lights on, but it was still light enough that that wasn't particularly unusual.

"Maybe they're upstairs, and it's taking them a while to come down," Elizabeth said.

Martha loved that Elizabeth was always so hopeful. She shook her head and pointed to the air conditioner that stuck out the front window. It was quiet.

"If anyone was home, they would be running that," she said.

Elizabeth took a deep breath and let it out slowly. "I guess you're right. She's not here."

Martha understood her disappointment. If Annalise had been here, they would know that she was safe. But seeing how empty this place was, all her own fears had come rushing back. Where was she?

Martha turned and looked around, taking in the barn, the quiet outbuildings, and the fields planted with soybeans and alfalfa. Then her eyes drifted down the long driveway to the road and settled on the black metal mailbox. Something about it tugged at her.

Then, with a start, she realized what it was.

CHAPTER EIGHTEEN

"Do you remember the names of all the people who bought linens at the shop?" Martha asked.

It took Elizabeth a minute to catch up with what her sister had said. Why was she asking that now?

"I think so," she said. The empty porch swing creaked as a light breeze rustled the chains. "There was Chrissy Peters and Janet Pelz and Diane Presley. And also Alma Yoder." Then, a moment later, "Why?"

"Look."

Elizabeth turned and looked down the driveway to see what Martha was pointing at. All that was there was a mailbox painted with what looked like a John Deere tractor. She squinted at it, and it took a moment before the letters registered. The name PELZ was written in white letters on the side.

"This must be where Janet Pelz lives," Martha said.

She understood now. Mary had come here to talk to Janet, but Janet hadn't been home. Looking around now, it sure didn't seem like anyone was.

"That might help explain how that receipt from the shop ended up in the front seat of the car Annalise was probably driving," Elizabeth said. "Annalise and Janet are related somehow."

"But it doesn't explain where she is, or where Janet is for that matter," Martha said. "Or how she's connected to

Jack DiNapoli. Or whether she's safe or why she left her phone behind."

It was all true, Elizabeth realized. They may have connected the dots that linked Annalise and Janet Pelz, but in the end it hadn't gotten them any closer to finding her. They had come here hoping for answers, but all they'd found were more questions.

"We'll find her," Martha said. "I know we will."

Elizabeth knew her sister was trying to make her feel better, and she appreciated it. But she didn't feel any better.

"I just can't help thinking that if the police could get into that phone, we'd find information that would lead us right to her," Elizabeth said.

Martha nodded. "John and his team are working on it. They're good at what they do. I'm sure they'll figure it out sooner or later."

Elizabeth scanned the yard, looking for anything, any clue that might help them figure out where Annalise had gone. Two newspapers lay on the porch, covered in the familiar blue bag that protected them from the rain. There were geraniums and pansies in ceramic pots on the porch. Judging by the wilted look of the petals, they hadn't been watered in several days. The bark around the trunk of a beautiful old elm had been damaged when something had been tied around it, she noticed. But the grass under it was fresh and green and even. They had had a dog once, but it had been many years ago, she gathered. There was a horseshoe hung over the barn door. She didn't see how any of this was helpful in finding what they needed.

Martha stepped off the porch and started to walk down the dirt driveway. Elizabeth watched her go, unsure of whether to follow her. What was she doing? She watched her sister march right down the driveway and open up the mailbox.

Oh, goodness. "Martha!"

Martha looked up. Elizabeth stepped off the porch and jogged out to where her sister was already riffling through the contents of the mailbox.

"What are you doing?" she called.

"Investigating," Martha said calmly, pulling out an armload of mail.

"You can't go through people's mailboxes. That's got to be illegal."

"It's no such thing," Martha said. "It's searching for clues."

"In their mailbox?" Elizabeth looked around. They were at the edge of the driveway, right on the road. Anyone driving past could see what she was doing. Or anyone in that house across the road.

Martha sorted through familiar envelopes from the electric company, seed catalogs, and solicitations for money from charities. She handed the magazines and a stack of mail to Elizabeth. There were new issues of *Cooking Light* and *Antique Power* and *Country* and *Consumer Reports*. *People,* addressed to Annalise. And there was a handwritten letter addressed to Phil Pelz from someone named Margaret Kearney, who lived in Edina, Minnesota.

"For one, their mailbox is far too full for this to just be one day's mail," Martha said, sorting through her stack.

"Maybe they just get a lot of mail," Elizabeth said.

Martha shook her head. "No one has been here for several days."

Elizabeth had a hard time arguing with that conclusion. The newspapers on the porch and the wilted flowers showed her sister was right.

"For another, they have family in Minnesota," Martha said.

"How do you know that letter is from family?"

"Who writes letters these days?"

Elizabeth shrugged.

"My money is on this being Phil's mother or aunt. Someone from the generation that still appreciates the value of a handwritten note. But in any case, we now know that someone named Phil Pelz lives here. And judging from the fact that this subscription to *Consumer Reports* is his, he's probably not a teenager. Maybe Annalise's father."

"Stepfather, more likely, judging by the last name."

He was also most likely fairly responsible and careful with his money, Elizabeth realized. But she still didn't understand how that got them closer to finding Annalise.

She gave the mail back to Martha, who pushed the armload of mail back into the mailbox. Elizabeth looked around, hoping no one had seen them commit what had to be a crime of some sort. There were no cars on the road, but a woman had emerged from the house across the street and was watching them.

"We should get out of here," Elizabeth said. Was she going to report them?

"Nonsense." Martha closed the mailbox and then turned and waved to the woman. "Let's go talk to her."

Before Elizabeth could figure out how to respond, Martha was already crossing the road. Elizabeth wasn't sure what else to do, so she followed a few steps behind her. The woman's house was a well-kept two-story with gingerbread trim and a beautiful oak in the yard. Flower beds planted along the slate walkway and next to the driveway bloomed with goldenrod, hollyhocks, phlox, and black-eyed Susans.

"Hi there." The woman in Bermuda shorts and a souvenir T-shirt from Alaska watched them approach. Elizabeth guessed she was perhaps ten years older than Martha, but it was hard to tell under her floppy hat.

"Hello." Martha stepped forward and held out her hand. "I'm Martha Watts, and this is my sister Elizabeth Classen. We run the shop Secondhand Blessings over on Ronks Road."

The woman nodded, but either that detail didn't register or else it did nothing to alleviate her suspicions. "Madeleine Valentine," she said simply.

"We're trying to get in touch with Annalise Waters," Martha continued. "Do you know the Pelz family?"

"Sure." She nodded. "Been living there for a long time. She was just a kid when her mom married Phil. Cute kid. Now she's almost grown up."

"Have you seen Annalise recently?" Martha asked. She was going to simply gloss over the fact that Madeleine had seen them going through the Pelzes' mail, Elizabeth saw. Well, they'd see how that went.

"Can't say I have." She had a pair of gardening shears in her hand, and gardening gloves peeked out of her pocket. "Haven't seen anyone around the place the last few days. I

208 | MYSTERIES of LANCASTER COUNTY

think the whole family is away at a wedding. Left Friday morning."

If that was the case, what had Annalise been doing by the side of the road Friday night?

"Are you sure?" Martha asked. "We have reason to believe Annalise was dropped off here Friday night."

"If she was, I didn't see her," Madeleine said. "There hasn't been anyone around that I've seen."

If she was right, that meant Walt Goodwin was lying about more than where he'd dropped her off.

"What is she like?" Elizabeth asked. "Do you know much about the family?"

"Yep." She shifted the shears from one hand to another. "Janet and I are very friendly. She checks in on me and Bradley. She thinks we're elderly, which is silly, but I will admit that it's nice. In the winter, they'll pick up stuff from the store for us so we don't have to go out on the icy roads." She used the back of her free arm to wipe beads of sweat from her brow, and Elizabeth noted that the suspicion she'd shown at first had seemed to dissipate. "Annalise is a nice kid. Used to be a tomboy, always running around with her older brother, shooting BB guns and riding ATVs, and fixing up old cars and tractors and what-all. But as she's grown up, we've seen her less and less. I guess she's busy with school and theater and work and all that."

"Where does she work?" They hadn't heard about a job yet.

"Over at Bookberries. Been working there a few months, I think. Savin' up for college, or so she says."

Elizabeth recognized the name of a bookstore in town.

"What do you mean, 'so she says'?"

"Oh, I don't know. Just that school never seemed to be her priority. Last time I heard, she was talking about going off to New York after high school and becoming an actress. Real practical career choice. But I guess that's what teenagers are like." She shifted her feet. "Sometimes it's hard to know about kids these days."

"Did you ever see her with people...well, people you wouldn't want your own daughter hanging out with?" Martha asked.

Madeleine inclined her head, and Martha explained. "My daughter Trish went through something of a wild streak in high school. I just wondered if Annalise had gone through something similar."

Elizabeth now saw where Martha was going with this. It was a fair question, though not one she'd expected.

"No, not that I ever saw," Madeleine said. "But then, she's always had a bit of an independent streak, so I guess I wouldn't be too surprised." After a pause, she added, "Apple doesn't fall far from the tree, I guess."

"What do you mean?" Elizabeth asked.

"Oh, I'm probably being unkind. Janet is lovely. So kind to me."

"But..." Martha was gently encouraging her to go on.

Madeleine paused for a moment and then said, "Well, Annalise and her brother had different fathers, and Phil is Janet's third husband. Though this one seems to have stuck, so who knows? Maybe things have settled down for her."

Elizabeth wasn't sure how this was relevant, and she felt bad listening to what sounded like gossip, so she tried to redirect the conversation.

"Did you ever see Annalise with a cell phone?"

"Sure. Kids these days never seem to be without them. Why?"

"Do you remember what it looked like?" Martha asked.

"Some horrible pink sparkly thing. She came over with her mom to bring us some beans from their garden last week and didn't put the thing down the entire time. Almost like she wasn't even here. I don't understand why this generation seems to think the people on their phone are more important than the people in front of you in real life, but they're all like that these days."

So it *was* Annalise's phone that they had found Friday night. Was she mistaken about Annalise not being here Friday night? It sure seemed like she knew just about everything that went on along this road. But if she was right, they were wrong. Elizabeth felt herself getting more and more confused. She wanted to ask more questions but couldn't think of what to say.

"Thank you for talking with us," Martha said. "You have been most helpful." She turned to go, and Elizabeth didn't know what else to do but follow her.

They walked a little way down the road, and Elizabeth could feel Madeleine watching them go.

"What do you think?" Elizabeth asked, jogging a bit to catch up with her sister. "Is she telling the truth?"

"I think she is," Martha said, turning to look both ways before she crossed the street. "But I also think there's something big we've missed."

"What could it be?" Elizabeth crossed the road behind her.

But instead of answering, Martha stopped dead in her tracks at the end of the Pelzes' driveway. Elizabeth hurried and stopped next to her.

"Elizabeth." Martha reached out and grabbed Elizabeth's arm. The sun was hanging lower in the sky now, and Martha's shadow stretched out over the yard.

"What is it?"

"Remember that article I read about the most common types of passcodes people use?"

"Yes." Elizabeth smoothed down a hair that had gotten caught in a cross breeze.

"It said that in addition to the more generic, obvious passcodes, people often use easily guessed codes like their birthday or the last four digits of their phone numbers. Or their address." Martha pointed toward the mailbox once again. There, underneath the name Pelz, were the numbers 1789.

It took Elizabeth a minute before she responded, but then her mouth dropped open. "You don't think..."

"I don't know," Martha said. "It's just a guess. But it seems like it might be worth trying."

Elizabeth let a slow smile spread across her face. "I think we need to give John another call."

John didn't answer his phone once again, so after they made a quick stop at Bookberries and spoke with the manager, Elizabeth dropped Martha off at home to have dinner with her family, then drove to John's house. The driveway was empty, and there were no lights on. She sat in her car in front of the house and tapped her fingers on the steering wheel. Where was he? He hadn't mentioned any plans when she'd talked to him earlier. For a brief moment, she worried that he might be out with someone else, taking some other woman to dinner, but then she realized she was being silly. John wouldn't—and even if he did want to take someone else out to dinner, there was no reason he couldn't. He could take whoever he wanted—

But she was wasting time now, worrying about things that didn't matter. John had been at work earlier, so that was the most logical place for him to be now. She put the car in gear, pulled away from his house, and headed toward the police station.

A few minutes later, Elizabeth walked inside the modern brick building and headed toward the front desk. A young woman in thick-framed glasses looked up as she entered.

"Hi there." Elizabeth had met Donna before; she was friendly and helpful and whip-smart. "I was hoping I could talk to John Marks."

Donna smiled and shook her head. "I'm afraid they're all in a big meeting right now. I'm not sure how much longer they'll be, but it's been going on a couple of hours."

"Oh." That would explain why John hadn't answered her calls before, she supposed. But she needed to talk to him. "Is the meeting about the missing girl and the phone?"

"I couldn't tell you, I'm afraid," Donna said.

It had to be, Elizabeth thought. What else could have John tied up for so long on a Sunday evening? But she had to get through to him. She had to tell him that they'd found out Annalise's name and where she lived, and possibly how to unlock the phone.

"Is there any way to get a message to him?" Elizabeth asked. "It's rather important."

"I'm afraid not," Donna said. "They specifically asked not to be disturbed."

Elizabeth was sure Martha would not let herself be shut down here. She somehow had a way of not taking no for an answer. But Elizabeth didn't know how to channel that power, so reluctantly, she said, "Will you let him know I need to talk to him as soon as he's free?"

"I sure will," Donna said.

Elizabeth nodded and, unsure what else to do, sat down in one of the chairs near the front door. At first she tried sending another text to John, telling him that she was in the lobby hoping to talk to him, in the hopes that he might see it and let her in, but there was no response. He must not have his cell phone with him in the meeting.

Elizabeth adjusted her position on the chair. It was hard molded vinyl, and not at all comfortable, but at least it was cool in here. She might as well use the time to see what she could learn about Walt Goodwin, she decided. There had to be a reason he had lied to them about where Annalise lived. But what was it? She pulled up a search window on her phone and ran a search for his name. She wasn't sure what she was hoping she would find, but the few hits that came up were pictures in the local paper he'd been tagged in for tractors he'd displayed at the county fair in previous years. He had some nice antiques, she had to admit. In a photo from the county fair three years back, he was posing in front of a fire-engine red International Harvester with huge back tires and smaller front wheels. It was a model 806, built in 1965, according to the caption under the photo. Elizabeth felt the familiar wave of sadness she often felt when she was reminded of her father. Daddy would have loved that tractor. But she couldn't see how these photos really helped her. She already knew that Walt was into antique tractors. That didn't explain why he would lie about Annalise.

Elizabeth had exhausted all the links that showed up when she searched for Walt's name, and she hadn't learned anything. It wasn't that surprising that there wasn't a lot about him online, she knew. People of her father's generation didn't put their whole lives online like kids did now. Daddy hadn't even had an email account, let alone a Facebook profile or Instagram account. She had to laugh when she imagined what he would have said about Twitter.

She looked up, but Donna was still typing on her computer, and there was no sign that the meeting inside the office had broken up.

Elizabeth wasn't sure what else to do, so she decided to use the time to try to get some more ideas for redecorating her room. She had liked Mary's suggestion of a more country look. She ran a search for "farmhouse decorating" and found Pinterest boards full of ideas. She liked some of the images of white-painted wood and iron bedsteads and clean, pale walls. But what was it with all the giant clocks on the walls? And why were there so many hand-lettered wooden signs saying things like *Home Is Where You Hang Your Hat* and *Farmhouse*? If you lived in one, like she did, you didn't really need to advertise it. And so much of the decor didn't make sense. Galvanized buckets holding plants hung on walls and blankets draped over ladders that went nowhere. If it wasn't useful, Elizabeth didn't have much patience for it.

Well, maybe farmhouse wasn't exactly the aesthetic she would go for. But there were elements she liked about the pictures she saw. It looked cozy, and that was what she wanted in her bedroom.

As she scrolled, a text message from Mary popped up. Elizabeth clicked on it and saw that it was a link to a website. A second later, another message followed.

I DID SOME RESEARCH INTO WALT GOODWIN. DO YOU THINK HE THINKS THE IRS AND THE POLICE ARE CONNECTED?

What in the world? Elizabeth had no idea what to make of that message, so she clicked on the link and studied the page that popped up. It was a chat page in some kind of online forum. She scrolled to the top and saw that it was a page on the website for *Antique Power* magazine. She'd seen a copy of the magazine in Phil's mailbox and knew it was a magazine all about antique tractors. Still, it took her a while to see what Mary had been getting at, but after she'd scrolled and read several of the threads, she understood. Was it really possible that—

"Elizabeth?"

She looked up and found John standing in the doorway that led to the back of the station.

"John." Elizabeth hopped up and tucked her phone into her purse.

"I'm sorry to keep you waiting. We were in an all-hands-on-deck meeting. I just got your messages and found out you've been waiting here for quite a while."

She glanced at her watch and realized it had been nearly an hour since she'd arrived. "That's all right." Elizabeth had so many questions, so many things she wanted to say, and she had to fight to keep them all from coming out at once. "Did you find her?"

"Not yet," John said. "Bu we're working on strategies to find out who she is and where she went."

He didn't know her name yet, then. Or, likely, where she lived, or worked, or what had really happened Friday night. Elizabeth thought she now knew the answers to most of those questions.

"I might be able to help you with that," Elizabeth said.

John tilted his head and gestured for her to follow him. "I'm all ears."

Twenty minutes later, Elizabeth was sitting across from John in a conference room in the back of the police station. He'd brought in Police Chief Bender, and several other members of the police force were gathered around the cell phone in the pink sparkly case. After it had lived so large in her mind these past few days, it was odd to see it in person again.

Elizabeth had told John what she'd learned, and they already had a team dispatched to the Pelz farm to gather information. Another officer was on the phone—Officer Stahl, she thought—who was trying to get ahold of Janet Pelz. It turned out that despite the long meeting, the police had not managed to learn Annalise's last name or where she lived or who her parents were, and they sat a bit sheepishly now,

about to try to unlock the phone again. Elizabeth found herself wondering what they *had* been talking about for so long,
but didn't dare ask. She knew they needed to hurry, and she
was grateful that so many officers were here on a Sunday evening, when surely most of them would rather be home with
their families. It was a sign of how seriously they were taking
this case.

"You are certain it was 1789?" the officer who had the
phone on the table in front of him said. She was pretty sure
he'd been introduced to her as Officer Martinez.

"I'm sure that was the address of the farm where she
lives," Elizabeth said. It was intimidating to be here surrounded by officers in dark blue uniforms. But she
reminded herself that she hadn't done anything wrong,
that she had figured out more than they had. "But I don't
know if that's the passcode to unlock the phone. That part
is just a hunch."

Chief Bender looked around the table. "How many attempts
have been made to unlock the phone so far?"

"Nine, sir," Officer Martinez said.

"And we don't know if the phone is set to erase all its contents after ten failed attempts to unlock it?" Chief Bender
asked.

"No, sir. There's no way to know that at this point."

Elizabeth understood then what was at stake here. There
was a chance that if they tried the address as the passcode and
they were wrong, the phone would erase all its contents and
eliminate any chance that they would be able to use it to locate
Annalise.

"Most people don't have such high safety protocols, as they're not the default set by the manufacturer," Officer Martinez said. "So the relative risk is low."

Chief Bender nodded. "Okay then. Try the code."

Elizabeth held her breath as Officer Martinez punched in the passcode. No one said anything as the screen seemed to freeze, but a moment later, a smile spread across his face. "We're in."

CHAPTER NINETEEN

The lasagna would be ready in five minutes, and Martha was hovering in the kitchen, trying to decide what to do. The garlic bread was ready to go in the oven, the salad was made, and the table set. She should be excited to sit down to Sunday dinner with Craig and his family. But she felt bad about what had happened with Kevin earlier, and she didn't know how to make it right.

He was in the next room, watching a TV show about monster trucks with Dylan. From one screen to another—but at least this one was shared by other people. Craig and Molly were taking a walk together to get some exercise.

Martha hovered in the doorway, unsure. Would he be upset if she interrupted him now? But wouldn't dinner be awkward if she didn't talk to him beforehand? He hadn't really even looked at her since their confrontation this afternoon.

Martha took a deep breath and made a decision. She was the adult here. She would need to step up and start this conversation, because Kevin wasn't going to do it.

"Kevin, could you come here a moment?"

She couldn't see his face, but he only waited a moment before he pushed himself up. "Coming."

He came into the kitchen and waited to hear what she had to say.

"I want to apologize."

Kevin didn't react.

"For how things went earlier."

Again, his face betrayed no emotion, and so she plowed on.

"It's just that, I used to see you all the time, whenever I wanted. I was part of your life and could come to your school concerts and hockey games and, well, just a normal Sunday dinner. I miss that."

Kevin nodded, slowly.

"I miss *you*. And I only get you for a week. I want to see you while you're here. It's just that, well, when you're absorbed in your phone, you're not really here."

"Mom already told me I had to keep my phone out of sight for the rest of the visit."

She had? This was news to Martha. When had she done that? She must have heard—or heard about—their conversation earlier. Martha was grateful. This was what she had wanted, after all.

"I appreciate that," she said, trying to keep her voice level. "And I'm glad. But, it's just that..." She was tripping over the words, trying to figure out how to say what she wanted to say. "I worry that you spend so much time talking to people virtually. I worry that you're not spending enough time connecting with people in the real world."

"They're real people, you know. They're just not right in front of me."

"I know that." And on one level, he was right. But on the other, he was missing the point entirely. She thought about quoting the statistics about how teen depression and suicide were up, engagement with actual communities, down. But that wasn't really what this was about.

She decided to try a different tactic. "When you're absorbed in your phone, I know that you're talking to your friends, and they're important to you."

Kevin nodded, uncertain.

"But it makes it feel like you're not interested in me and in the other people around you." Martha had to bite down after she said the words to fight back the tears that unexpectedly sprang up. She wasn't usually able to be so candid, and saying what was really on her heart made her feel vulnerable.

"But I am," Kevin said. "I can care about you and also talk to my friends."

"I'm sure that's true." Martha tried to phrase her words carefully. "But that's not what it feels like to me. To me, it feels like you would rather talk to your friends than talk to me. And I get it. Your friends probably are more fun than I am, and care about the same things you do, and all that. But when you're talking to them instead of talking to me, it really makes me feel like you don't want to be here."

Part of her couldn't believe she was talking like this to her grandson. Wasn't it just yesterday that he was a toddler, following her around in diapers?

"But I do want to be here. My phone doesn't have anything to do with that."

Why wasn't he getting it? Was it that hard to understand that she wanted to spend her limited time with him actually *with* him?

"But it feels like it does to me," she said. "It feels like you would rather talk to them than me. And you'll see them again in a week. But once you go home on Saturday, I don't know when I'll see you again." The family was going to see Molly's parents at Christmas. "And, as it turns out, I really like you. I would love to actually get to be with you while I have the chance."

Kevin didn't say anything, but he did step forward and give her a hug. He didn't say he understood, or apologize, or make any promises. But Martha supposed that wasn't likely from a teen boy anyway. She understood that this was his way of saying all of that.

"Okay," he said.

And that was good enough.

After they'd gotten the phone unlocked, everyone in the room started to rush around, shouting instructions and suggestions, and they seemed to forget that Elizabeth was there. She sat quietly at the conference room table in the back of the police station, watching the officers jockey for the attention of Martinez, who held the phone in his hand.

In a matter of minutes, the police chief had sent officers off to call the mysterious Viv—whose last name, they discovered, was Thompson—with the phone number for her they'd found listed in Annalise's contacts. He'd also dispatched an officer to call Jack DiNapoli, again using his number from the phone. And they'd found Annalise's own phone number and had someone on the line with the phone company, trying to get her phone records pulled to see if they could figure out whether she'd tried to find her phone and, if so, where she'd been at the time.

Elizabeth watched the officers swirling around her, talking over each other. Somehow it was both chaotic and well-orchestrated at the same time. Someone was suggesting they check to see if Annalise had used Location Services to find her missing phone, and they discovered that Location Services had been turned off. Someone else suggested that they go through her photos to see if there were any clues there. Elizabeth watched John, moving with easy grace as he interacted with his peers. He was calm, steady, respectful of the other officers and their ideas. He was exactly who you'd want to be around in an emergency, Elizabeth thought. She watched as they all moved under the fluorescent lights.

As she watched, theories ran through her head, and she played them out, one at a time. She tried to piece together what they'd heard had happened Friday night, and what she'd learned at the Pelz farm today, and what she'd discovered by talking to the owner of the bookstore. Elizabeth pulled out her phone and did an internet search for Vivian Thompson. And then, it all started to become clear.

Just as she figured out what had really happened, Officer Stahl came back into the room and announced, "We got her. We know where she is."

CHAPTER TWENTY

Elizabeth hadn't been given permission to hop into the police car with John, exactly. It was more that she'd simply walked out to the parking lot with the rest of the officers and climbed into the back seat, and no one had questioned it. Officer Stahl had joined John in the passenger seat of the cruiser, and he'd given her a glance, but then he'd seemed to accept that she'd be riding along, the same way John had. Maybe they were wordlessly acknowledging the important role she'd played in bringing them all to this point. Maybe they'd agreed that it would be good to have her along in case any more puzzles came up, since she and her sisters seemed to have more luck solving them than the officers themselves had. Maybe they were just too excited to argue. But whatever the reason, here she was in the back seat while John drove the police cruiser— one in a line of a half dozen—east along the Old Philadelphia Pike, lights flashing.

As they drove, John explained to Officer Stahl that after talking to Vivian Thompson and Jack DiNapoli and Janet Pelz, the police had pieced together what had really happened, just as Elizabeth had.

Annalise Waters was seventeen, and though she wouldn't graduate from high school until next year, she was itching to get off the farm and to the big city, John explained. She wanted to pursue acting and had dreams of making it big on Broadway.

"Her dreams were fueled by her friend Vivian, who graduated from Conestoga Valley a year ago and moved to New York," Elizabeth added from the back seat. "Annalise talked a great deal about Vivian at work, so Melanie told me. Vivian seems to have had some success, with parts in choruses and bit parts in commercials, that sort of thing."

"That's right," John said. "Annalise had kept in touch with her, and it seems that she reached out to her recently about coming to New York to look for acting work."

"But she still had another year of high school," Officer Stahl said. His strawberry-blond hair and fair skin had a bluish tint in the dark police cruiser.

"It seems she decided she didn't want to wait," John said. "Her brother Jack had gone off to college a year ago, and she'd been less and less content being stuck on a farm in the middle of nowhere, according to Jack. Jack didn't come home from college for the summer, which made things worse, but their mother told us Annalise had been acting strangely since school ended anyway."

"Strange how?" Office Stahl asked.

"Her mother said she'd been quiet and secretive, and wasn't spending money like she used to. She wasn't coming home with new clothes and things like she had been every payday. Janet didn't really think anything of it, though."

"Annalise had come up with a plan," Elizabeth said. "There was a family wedding coming up, and she knew her parents would be out of town, and she saw an opportunity."

"How did she get out of going to the wedding?" Officer Stahl asked.

"She had to work, apparently," John said. "Over at Book-berries."

"She was scheduled to work Sunday," Elizabeth said. "I spoke to Melanie Granger, the owner, this afternoon."

"Her plan was to leave town Friday evening, just a little while after her parents left for the wedding in Cincinnati," John continued. "But she only got a couple of miles before her car broke down. Jack owned the car, but he had left it at home for the summer for his sister to use, and he told us it broke down often."

Some car to leave for your sister, Elizabeth thought, but she kept quiet. Annalise was probably still grateful for it.

"The car that was found on Weavertown Road Saturday morning," Officer Stahl said, nodding.

Cornfields and farms zoomed past the windows as they raced along the rural road. Up ahead, the lights of Intercourse, the neighboring small town, were just visible.

"Exactly," John continued. "Elizabeth and her sisters were the first to put that together." He met her eyes in the mirror and then looked back at the road. "Annalise must have realized that she wasn't going to get to New York that night, and we think she must have decided to walk home."

"But it was dark," Officer Stahl said.

"Right. And there are no streetlights out that way," John said. "So she used her phone as a flashlight. Walt Goodwin saw it, and stopped to offer her a ride home."

"Why didn't she come back the next day and retrieve her phone?" Stahl asked. "She must have missed it right away."

"I think she meant to drop it," Elizabeth said. "She probably didn't want to be tracked. If you're trying to disappear, what better way than to get rid of the device that tracks your every move?" No one had yet acknowledged out loud that they weren't thinking of this as a kidnapping any longer, but there it was.

"It's a good theory," John said. He slowed as they approached a car going much slower than they were. John looked at it, and seeing that it was a blue sedan, he passed it without a backward glance. It wasn't the black sports car they were looking for.

"But I thought she had Location Services turned off," Stahl said. "Wouldn't that mean no one could use her phone to track her?"

"It would mean that no one could use Find My iPhone or a similar location-tracking service to find her," John said. "But any texts or calls or data she used would still be transmitted over a wireless network, and we would be able to track which cell towers those were routed through."

Elizabeth had heard about this on a television news show. When you made a call on a cell phone, the signal was routed to the nearest cell tower. Using that information, the phone company could find your general area. From what she'd heard, it was tricky to get specific information about a person's location in a city with multiple cell towers, but they probably could have found out whether Annalise was in the general Lancaster area or another state entirely. And they all believed now that another state had been her plan all along.

"But then why would she turn the SOS function on?" John asked.

Elizabeth had to admit, that part didn't add up.

"And really. Have you ever seen a teenager get rid of a cell phone? I think my daughter's is superglued to her hand," Officer Stahl said.

"What's the alternative?" John asked.

Officer Stahl thought for a moment. "She got scared. A young girl walking alone at night. A truck slows down and stops, and a man leans out. It could be scary."

"It's possible," John said. "But have you seen Walt Goodwin? He's not exactly Freddy Krueger." It was hard to imagine that seeing Walt would frighten the girl.

"So what do you think?" Officer Stahl asked.

After a pause, John said, "She just dropped it."

They both stared at him.

"Okay, I know it sounds unlikely, but hear me out," John said. "It was dark, her big escape plan had been foiled, she was excited that someone had saved her the trouble of walking several miles along dark roads. In her excitement to get into the truck, it slipped out of her hand."

"And somehow turned itself to blink on and off in the process?" Stahl asked.

"The SOS button is there on the screen. It's possible."

"It's difficult to imagine," Elizabeth said. She tried to picture it, and as she played the scenario through in her mind a few times, she realized that it wasn't crazy. It was certainly possible, even if unlikely. "But then, haven't you ever left your phone behind by accident?" She had left her phone charging on the counter when she'd thought it was in her purse, or in her car when she thought she'd brought it in. In her case, it was a minor nuisance, but she could see how it might have happened.

"Sure," Officer Stahl said, "but not while I was using it as a flashlight on a deserted road. So you're saying, what, she just dropped it and turned it to blink SOS by accident on the way down?" He shook his head. "I guess we can ask her more about it when we find her, but it's at least more likely than the theory that she got rid of her phone on purpose. I'm telling you, a teenager would never do that."

John looked dubious, and Elizabeth had to admit it was a flimsy theory, but she could also see Officer Stahl's point, that most teens—even teens running off to start a new life—would be unlikely to leave their phones behind.

"Okay, so for whatever reason, Annalise leaves her phone behind when she gets in the car Friday night," Officer Stahl said. "And Walt drove her home. But he didn't, right?"

"I think he actually did drive her to her home," John said. "He just didn't want us to find out where he'd dropped her off."

"But why would he lie about that?" Officer Stahl was shaking his head again. "It doesn't make any sense."

"Actually, I have an idea about why he lied," Elizabeth said.

Both officers waited for her to go on.

"My sister Mary found that Walt's been active in a forum on an antique tractor magazine site. I have no idea how she found it, but Mary can get ridiculously focused when it's something she's interested in."

She could see in the rearview mirror that John was skeptical, and she could see why. But she pressed on.

"It was a forum where they were talking about charging and paying sales tax when you sell an antique tractor. I knew that Walt Goodwin was a collector, because that's how he knew my dad. And I found out that Phil Pelz was into collecting antique tractors when we were at his house."

"Collecting antique tractors? Is that a thing?" Stahl asked. Elizabeth didn't know him well, but his Brooklyn accent made it seem unlikely he'd lived in the area for long.

"It is indeed," Elizabeth said. "A popular thing around these parts."

"How did you discover that Phil Pelz was into collecting antique tractors?" John asked.

"He had a tractor painted on his mailbox, and he subscribed to *Antique Power* magazine. My dad got that, so I recognized it. It's about collecting antique tractors. But also, he had a heavy equipment trailer for towing antiques to fairs. Daddy had one of those too."

"Okay," Officer Stahl said. "So he collected old tractors. So what does that have to do with anything?"

"Sales tax," Elizabeth said. At their blank looks, she realized she needed to elaborate. "Apparently, when you sell something at an auction, they add tax onto the sale price, so the buyer has to pay more, and the seller has to report that income to the IRS. So a number of collectors try to use back channels to buy and sell equipment."

"Back channel antique tractors?" Office Stahl asked. He looked like he wanted to burst out laughing.

"I suppose it's more like direct sales, one collector to another," Elizabeth said.

"Okay..." Officer Stahl still looked skeptical.

"Mary found someone using the screen name WGoodwin-BiH discussing what would happen if you got caught not charging sales tax."

"Walt Goodwin, Bird-in-Hand," John said.

"So you think Walt wasn't charging sales tax, and that's why he lied to the police?" Officer Stahl frowned.

"I think he must have sold a tractor to Phil Pelz," Elizabeth said. "Based on the photos in the online newspaper I found. A couple of years ago Walt was standing in front of a Farmall at the county fair, and this past year, Phil Pelz was standing in front of it."

"And you think he got scared when we came around asking about the Pelz family," John said.

"Because he thought you guys were the IRS?" Stahl still didn't believe it. Well, it was hard to believe. And maybe she was way off base.

"I think it's possible. That's all I'm saying. It's a possible explanation. I know you all think the police and the IRS have nothing in common, but to the average citizen, the government is the government. Why wouldn't the IRS send police officers to arrest you if you cheated on your taxes?"

"That's not how it—"

"I know," Elizabeth said. "I'm just saying it might be what went through Walt's panicked mind when a police car showed up at his place, and we started asking about Annalise. It was already on his mind, obviously, based on his forum questions, so it's possible."

"We'll know more once we find Annalise," John said. "And find out what her side of the story is. We can talk to Walt again too."

"All right." That seemed to pacify Officer Stahl, who still didn't seem convinced. "Anyway. Whatever happened, you're saying that Annalise somehow made it home Friday night. But I thought you said you went to her place, and no one had been home for several days."

"It sure didn't look like anyone had," Elizabeth agreed. "Because no one had brought in the mail or watered the plants. But how likely is it that a teenager would do those things?"

"I know my daughter wouldn't," Officer Stahl said.

"It's possible she had been home, and we just assumed no one had been there." Elizabeth hated to think they'd led the investigation astray with false assumptions.

"So, okay, Walt Goodwin drops her off at her home Friday night," Officer Stahl said. "Somehow the nosy old neighbor lady misses that, and because there are no cars in the driveway, everyone thinks no one is home. But then what happened? Where *is* Annalise?"

"Sometime on Saturday morning she got the car started," John said, not answering his question.

"By herself?" Stahl asked.

"The neighbor lady Madeleine said she'd grown up working on cars with her older brother," Elizabeth said. They were flying down the road faster than was safe on these country roads. But hopefully the blaring siren and flashing lights would warn others to stay out of their way, and she knew time was of the essence.

"She used a credit card at Sheldon's Auto Parts Saturday morning," John said. "Her brother told us the fan belt was wonky, so likely that's what she bought. Must have ridden a bike or hitched a ride or something to get there."

"How do you know she went there?" Elizabeth asked.

"She had a credit card connected to her phone. Once we got into the phone, the credit card notifications from yesterday were there on the screen."

Elizabeth continued to be surprised by how much of their lives people put on their phones these days. "Her card connected to her phone? Why would you want to do that?"

"Oh, I have that on my phone," Officer Stahl said. "My daughter has access to my credit card for emergencies. This way I can see what 'emergencies' pop up for her. Last week there was apparently an emergency that necessitated a trip to Sephora." He shook his head.

Elizabeth thought about this, and she supposed she could see the benefit, but it also seemed invasive to her. Didn't people worry about what would happen if their phones fell into the wrong hands? Then again, that was what passcodes were supposed to protect against.

Elizabeth thought about the timing. If what John said was true, Annalise must have repaired the car between the time Martha reported seeing the car and the time the police arrived, probably an hour later. She had no idea how long a fan belt took to replace, but she supposed if Annalise knew what she was doing it must be possible.

But something else was bothering her as well. Something about what John had said.

"You said credit card notification*s*."

He met her eyes in the mirror again, a smile on his face.

"The second notification was from a Verizon store in Lancaster Saturday afternoon. For nearly four hundred dollars."

Elizabeth understood what that meant. "She bought a new phone."

John nodded. "Most likely."

Whether she'd left the phone on purpose or by accident, it seemed she'd decided to replace it before she made her next move.

"Okay, so by Saturday afternoon, she has her car repaired and her phone replaced. She must have left town then."

"You'd think so," John said. "But it turns out she decided to stick around a day and go to work."

"What in the world?" Officer Stahl was incredulous. "Instead of running away to be an actress, she decided to wait and do one more shift at the neighborhood bookstore? That doesn't make any sense."

"It doesn't make any sense unless you think about what day of the month it is," Elizabeth said. She'd figured this part out when she went to talk to Melanie at the bookstore earlier.

"It's the fifteenth," Officer Stahl said. "Why does that matter?"

"It's payday," Elizabeth said. "If Annalise went in and did her shift, she could pick up her pay from the past two weeks. Apparently she'd been considering that a loss when she'd planned to leave Friday night, but after spending nearly four hundred dollars on a new phone, she must have reconsidered."

"So you talked to her boss at the bookstore today?" Officer Stahl was looking at John.

"Elizabeth did that," John said.

"Melanie confirmed that Annalise left with a check when her shift ended at six this evening," Elizabeth said.

"And then what?" Stahl asked.

John shrugged. "And then she deposited the check—her mom has access to her bank account and confirmed that—and she called Vivian, otherwise known as Viv."

"Her friend in New York," Stahl said.

"That's right. And Vivian confirmed that Annalise was on her way."

"On her way where?"

Elizabeth looked at Officer Stahl in the dim blue light. Had he really not figured this out yet?

"New York," John said. He pressed his foot down on the gas, and the odometer inched past eighty. "And if we hurry, we can catch her before she crosses the state line."

Annalise was a minor. Elizabeth wasn't sure exactly what the laws were, but these officers were acting as if they could bring her home if they caught up with her before she left the state. Once she crossed the line, they had no jurisdiction to stop her.

"How do you know which way she's going?" Officer Stahl asked. "There are a hundred roads she could take to get to New York from here."

"That's true," John said. "There are a number of ways she could have gone. But really, it's only likely she would have taken one in particular."

"Which one?"

"How does your daughter know how to get where she wants to go?" John asked.

Officer Stahl chuckled. "She doesn't have a clue. She wouldn't be able to get to her school if she didn't follow the directions Google gave her."

John nodded to his phone, which was sitting on the console between them. There was a map on the screen, and John was following along the path it had laid out for them.

"That's how I get to unfamiliar places too," John said. "I type the address into Google Maps and go wherever it tells me to go."

Officer Stahl was nodding now. "And chances are, Google gave you the same directions it gave to Annalise."

"Based on when she deposited the paycheck, we think she had about a half hour head start," John said.

Officer Stahl looked grim. "Which means we'd better hurry."

The landscape was different out here, with tree-covered hills and dramatic vistas. The road was getting more crowded as the population grew, and they had to slow down significantly, but cars still moved out of their way, and both officers studied each one, looking for the black Camaro. If she hadn't been so tense, Elizabeth would have really enjoyed the sensation of traffic parting ahead of them.

"Can you really stop her though?" Elizabeth felt silly asking after all this. They had come all this way—obviously the officers must think they would be able to.

"Ultimately, no," John said. "If she's determined to move to New York and become an actress, she'll do it one way or another. But her parents are distraught, as you can imagine. She's seventeen, has very little money, and is running off to the biggest city in the nation to live with a friend they only vaguely know, hoping to make it in a field that's notoriously difficult."

Elizabeth may not have children of her own, but she could still imagine the fear and pain that scenario would inflict on any parent.

"She is young and naive, and even if we can't ultimately stop her, we can at least bring her home to her parents now. Maybe they can convince her to stay home until she graduates from high school."

The road hugged a river, with tall hills on both sides, and they passed under a beautiful arched stone bridge. Signs above the highway boasted of locations in New Jersey in the next few miles. The line of cars pulled over ahead of them, and John slowed as he passed them.

"Come on, come on," he said under his breath.

"Wait." Officer Stahl pointed. "Up there. Is that it?"

He was pointing at a car that was pulling over to the side of the road ahead of them. It was a black sports car. "Can you read the plates?" Officer Stahl squinted at the license plate, and John said, "That's it."

He used his radio to signal the other cars in the line, and somehow, following some choreography she didn't understand, the squad cars surrounded the black car.

"We'll be right back." John turned and gave Elizabeth a serious look. "Stay right here."

Elizabeth promised she would stay put, but as he closed the door, she realized that her promise was unnecessary. The back doors of the squad car didn't have handles on the inside. She couldn't get out if she tried.

Elizabeth couldn't hear what the officers were saying, but she could see John leaning in the front window and Officer

Stahl on the passenger side. The other officers stayed in their cars with the lights flashing.

John talked to the driver—Annalise, Elizabeth was sure— for what seemed like an hour, but was probably no more than ten minutes. And then, slowly, so slowly she wasn't sure she was really seeing it at first, Elizabeth saw Annalise emerge from the car. Elizabeth recognized her immediately, with the shoulder-length brown hair and her pretty heart-shaped face. She was crying, no doubt scared out of her mind by the fleet of police cars that flanked her. But she was nodding, and held on to John's arm in a way that made Elizabeth think he had gotten through to her.

As she watched Annalise get into a squad car, Elizabeth's thoughts went to another girl, one who went missing so many years ago. She said a prayer for Amber's family, wherever they were, that they had somehow found a measure of peace.

John talked to her a while longer, and then he turned to his car, looking in the windshield. Elizabeth knew he was looking for her. She waved, though she had no idea whether he could actually see her. But when he smiled and flashed a thumbs-up, Elizabeth felt an unexpected rush of tears, and tension she hadn't realized she'd been holding in her shoulders released.

She knew what John was trying to tell her.

They'd done it.

Annalise was coming home.

CHAPTER TWENTY-ONE

Elizabeth wasn't sure how late it was when she finally sat down with her sisters and John at the kitchen table that night. After they'd escorted Annalise home and talked with her family and reported in at the station, John had brought Elizabeth home. When the cruiser pulled into their driveway, Elizabeth saw Martha and Kevin coming to the house from the barn. They were both laughing, and Kevin was talking and waving his arms. Elizabeth didn't know what had him so excited, but she was thrilled to see them together with no phones in sight. Both Martha and Mary soon joined Elizabeth and John at the scarred kitchen table, where John confirmed that Annalise had indeed been planning to move to New York but had been having second thoughts the closer she got.

"It almost seemed like she was relieved when we caught her," he said, sipping the mint tea Martha had prepared. "I think the reality of what she was planning to do was hitting her."

"I'm sure seeing a line of police cars race up behind her didn't hurt," Mary said. "That would scare anybody straight."

Craig and Molly and the kids had gone upstairs, and the house was quiet, with just the hum of the window units in the peaceful night.

"I suspect she and her family will be having many long conversations in the near future," John said. "But she's home safe, for now at least."

"Did you ever find out why she left her phone behind?" There were slices of glazed lemon-blueberry bread on plates in front of each of them, and Martha used her fork to break off a bite.

"As unlikely as it sounds, she said she must have dropped it," John said. "She thinks it must have fallen when she was climbing into the truck. And she didn't realize she'd lost it until Walt dropped her at home." He blew on the tea, creating little ripples across the surface. He'd already polished off his slice of cake. "When she went back to look for it in the morning, it was gone."

"Because we found it," Elizabeth said. "If we'd simply left it there, she would have found it, and none of this would have happened."

"It's hard to say what would have happened," John said. "Maybe she'd be in New York right now. Or maybe she'd have given up and realized she was making a mistake much sooner."

"So she dropped the phone," Mary said. "And neither of them noticed the light at the side of the road?"

"It was behind them, I suppose," John said. "I have to believe her about that, because I don't honestly think she intended to leave her phone behind."

Elizabeth was pretty sure he was right about that. But there was still one thing she didn't understand. "So what was the SOS signal about?"

"Annalise said she didn't even realize the app did that." He pulled out his own phone and opened up the flashlight app he'd downloaded. There was what looked like a lifeguard's buoy beneath the main button. Elizabeth had seen one like it on the app she'd downloaded on her own phone. "My best guess is that she hit it accidentally," John said. "She doesn't seem to have done that on purpose either."

Part of Elizabeth couldn't believe it. It was all so unlikely, so unbelievable. After all the investigating, all the lies, everything, to have this whole thing be caused by a slip of the hand, a simple mistake...And yet...maybe it had been a good thing after all. If the phone hadn't been blinking, if it hadn't seemed so out of place out there on that country road, would Annalise have ended up making the biggest mistake of her life?

There was no way to know.

"So it happened like Walt Goodwin said it did after all," Mary said.

"Well, sort of," John confirmed. "He definitely did lie about where he dropped her off. But a team of officers went over to his place tonight, and he admitted he was scared that we would find out he knew Phil Pelz. He was afraid we'd somehow find out that he'd sold a tractor to Phil and didn't report the income."

"So he lied to the police to avoid getting in trouble for lying on his taxes?" Martha asked.

"It sounds really bad when you say it like that," Mary said.

"It is. We could have saved so much time if he'd simply told the truth about where he dropped Annalise off."

"I think we managed to convince him that we are not with the IRS," John said. "But my guess is that he'll be reporting his tractor sales on his tax returns from now on."

242 | MYSTERIES of LANCASTER COUNTY

Just then Mary yawned. Elizabeth looked up at the clock and was startled to see that it was after eleven. "We need to get to bed," she said. She still had so many questions, so many details she wanted to confirm so she could get the whole story straight in her mind. But they had to work in the morning, and John needed to get home too. There would be time to have all her questions answered tomorrow. Reluctantly, she pushed herself up.

"Thank you for your help putting the pieces together," John said, standing. "To all of you. We probably would have figured it all out eventually, but you sure sped things along."

Elizabeth felt a strange sort of satisfaction as she walked John to the door. There had been no kidnapping after all, and Annalise was home safely. As John had said earlier, they hadn't necessarily stopped Annalise from moving to New York altogether. If that was her dream, she would go there eventually. But she was only seventeen. Too young to be out on her own, and they had at least brought her back home safely tonight.

"I'll give you a call in the morning," John said. Elizabeth nodded and felt a thrill of expectation. If John said he would call, she knew he would indeed.

"I'll talk to you tomorrow," she said. She watched out the front window as he turned the car around, drove down the driveway, and pulled onto Classen Road. Then she turned and headed up the stairs. She brushed her teeth and changed into her pajamas, then stood next to her bed, looking around the tidy room. The wallpaper was still peeled off the corner in large swaths, and the plaster underneath was starting to bubble. It would need to be removed, and soon, but as Elizabeth took in the mantel, the large windows, the creaky wooden floor, she knew exactly how she wanted to redecorate the space.

"Are you envisioning how that wall would look with shiplap on it?"

Elizabeth gasped and whipped around. "You have to stop sneaking up on people like that."

"I didn't sneak up on anyone," Mary protested. "I even knocked on the door, but you were so absorbed you didn't hear."

Elizabeth sighed. "I guess I was kind of lost in my own thoughts."

"I have no idea what that's like," Mary said, smiling.

Elizabeth laughed. No one could lose herself like Mary could.

"So what were you thinking?" Mary asked. "Shiplap, or no?"

Elizabeth took in a deep breath and let it out slowly. "Actually, I was thinking about how much things had changed in the past year."

Rachel had made her see it first. That the reason she felt paralyzed about the decision of how to decorate her room had almost nothing to do with decor at all. That the reason she couldn't decide between mid-century and country charm and Victorian wasn't because she was indecisive about decorating style. She'd never had trouble making up her mind in the past. This whole thing was about something else entirely.

Mary stepped into the room and slipped an arm around Elizabeth's shoulders. The scent of her lotion wafted up, and it smelled familiar and comforting.

"It's been an adjustment for you, having us back, hasn't it?" she asked.

"It's been great. Don't get me wrong. I couldn't be happier about having you and Martha here again," Elizabeth said. "It's just that...Well, for so long, I knew who I was and what my role was. I took care of Mama. I knew my place and what was expected of me. But now that Mama is gone, and you're both here..." Oh dear. She was making a mess of this. "Again, it is such a gift to have you and Martha back. But I guess I'm still trying to figure out who I am now that it's the three of us again, and what my role is."

Mary pulled her arm off Elizabeth's shoulders and turned to face her. "You're trying to figure out who you are?" she asked.

"I mean..." How could she explain this? "I guess..."

"I'll tell you who you are," Mary said. "First of all, you are a beloved child of God. Next, you are my smart, strong, kind, dependable, sacrificial older sister. The one who has held this family together for the past few decades. The reason we're all still here."

"I—" Elizabeth started, but nothing else came out as she bit down to force back tears.

"Martha and me moving back home doesn't change the fact that you are the one who has run this farm and cared for this home and invested in this community all these years," Mary said. "I know you don't get enough credit for that, but Martha and I both know that you are the reason any of us—and this house—is still here. Our coming home doesn't change that. You are exactly who you have always been, even if it's hard to see that in the midst of all these changes."

On one level, Elizabeth knew Mary was right. The fact that her sisters were home didn't change anything. But at the same time, Mary had to see that it changed everything. And that, Elizabeth realized, wasn't a bad thing at all. Quite the opposite, in fact.

"I take it that means no to the shiplap," Mary said after a pause.

Elizabeth laughed. "That means no to the shiplap."

"Oh." Mary shook her head. "I see now. I know what you're going to do." She let out a long sigh.

"You know me too well," Elizabeth said.

"You're going to redo your room in the exact same plain old boring style, aren't you?"

"I'm going to make it even more boring," Elizabeth said. "Once that wallpaper is gone, I'm thinking of painting the walls a nice clean white."

"You're not keeping all this old furniture, are you?" Mary gestured at the dresser.

"Why not? It's good quality, in good condition. I like the clean, simple lines."

"Can I tempt you to paint it? Or give it a more updated shade of stain?" Mary ran her hand along the orangey bedside table.

"I don't think updated is really my thing," Elizabeth said. "And that's okay. I like being plain old simple me. It's familiar, and it's worked for me so far."

Elizabeth looked around the room that had been hers for so much of her life. She had used and loved the sturdy, simple furniture that served her so well, and she saw no reason to change that now. With everything else changing, this was one thing that could stay the same. It might be boring, but it was her.

Mary looked like she wanted to say so many things, but in the end, what she said was, "At least let me help you pick out a nice shade of white."

Elizabeth laughed. "How many shades of white can there possibly be?"

"Oh, my dear. You have so much to learn."

Elizabeth smiled. "All right. I'll let you help pick out a white. I can't stop you from being you, after all. As long as you'll let me be me."

Mary snaked her arm around her sister's shoulders once again and pulled her in for a hug. "There is no one else I'd rather have you be."

Elizabeth knew that Mary meant it, and she loved her for it. Her life might look nothing like it had a year ago, but it was so much better. Mary and Martha had come home, and she couldn't think of anything she would rather have than her sisters by her side.

A NOTE FROM THE AUTHOR

I came up with this story idea in the least Amish way possible: riding home from work on the New York City subway. A man was looking at his phone, and it started to flash a light out the camera lens. It made me remember that I have a flashlight app that does that, and it made me think how I'd always wondered in what context anyone would possibly need an SOS flare on their phone. By the time I got to my stop, the germ of the story was already brewing.

Although I suspect I'm actually a Martha, I related to Elizabeth a lot in this story, as she is struggling to find a design style that suits her. My husband and I recently renovated our Brooklyn townhouse, which was built in 1901 and had been altered with some questionable design and safety choices throughout the years. We wanted to stay true to the house's history, yet create a design and a style that worked for our active family. The question of what kinds of cabinet faces we liked somehow always seemed to devolve into questions about who we are as a family and how we want to live. Our homes say so much about what's important to us, and it was fun to explore Elizabeth's angst as she viewed her life through the lens of redecorating.

I hope you enjoy reading this book as much as I enjoyed writing it!

Beth Adams

ABOUT THE AUTHOR

Beth Adams lives in Brooklyn, New York, with her husband and two young daughters. When she's not writing, she spends her time cleaning up after two devious cats and trying to find time to read mysteries.

BARN FINDS

In this story, Mary becomes intrigued by a hand-stitched sampler made by a young girl in the latter part of the nineteenth century. Samplers of this sort were very common at this time, where a girl's skill with a needle was highly valued. Often these samplers were very detailed and elaborately worked, showing off a girl's stitching and design sensibilities.

The earliest known American sampler is from about 1645, and was made by Loara Standish of the Plymouth Colony. By the 1700s, young women created samplers depicting alphabets and numerals to learn the basic needlework skills needed at the time. By the latter part of the eighteenth century and into the nineteenth century, many girls were trained to make elaborate pieces with decorative motifs such as verses, flowers, and houses. The National Museum of American History has a wonderful collection of these samplers, and you can see a number of beautiful pieces on their website: http://americanhistory.si .edu/collections/object-groups/american-samplers.

A sampler in good condition that was created in the latter half of the nineteenth century would be quite valuable, but their value lies not so much in what price they would fetch but in what they tell us about life in centuries past.

FRESH FROM MARTHA'S KITCHEN

Martha's Meat Loaf
This is Craig's favorite!

1½ pounds ground beef
1 package onion soup mix
1 small onion
⅓ cup instant oatmeal
  (unflavored)

⅓ cup Italian bread crumbs
1 tablespoon mustard
1 tablespoon ketchup
1 egg

Combine all ingredients in a large bowl and put into greased loaf pan. Bake at 350° for 45 minutes to an hour. Serve piping hot!

Read on for a sneak peek of another exciting book
in the Mysteries of Lancaster County series!

Stamp of Approval
by Anne Marie Rodgers

Mary Classen Baxter lifted her face to the morning sun, enjoying its warmth as she strolled along the quarter-mile lane leading from her home to the barn where Secondhand Blessings, the thrift store and gift shop she and her sisters had reopened a few months ago, was located. It was temperate and sunny, a typical August morning in the charming southeastern Pennsylvania community of Bird-in-Hand, although Mary knew both the temperature and the humidity would climb as the day matured.

The old Victorian home she shared with her sisters was set back from the road on a slight rise while the barn had been built at the bottom of the hill. Her sisters, Elizabeth and Martha, were looking over a slight discrepancy in yesterday's deposit, so Mary had volunteered to come down and open the store.

Bees buzzed in the deep blue bellflowers lining the edges of the lane, while ragweed, thistle, and Queen Anne's lace choked the fencerows. Monarch butterflies floated gracefully from one clump of milkweed to another, and goldenrod still cast its brilliant glow in swaths of color through the uncultivated fields. She hadn't seen big groups of monarchs in years, she realized, and she recalled reading about the massive decline of the majestic insects' population. Looking at the peaceful scene as she walked, Mary couldn't help but assess it through an artist's eye. Perhaps she should paint the fields from this angle, while there still were some monarchs left to include in her paintings.

"Good morning, Mary."

Jolted from her musings, Mary waved and smiled as she unlocked and opened the outer barn doors and then punched the keypad that would unlock the interior door. "Good morning, Clea. Am I late?" She was almost certain it was still a few minutes before ten, the time the shop opened. Almost sure, she thought ruefully. Punctuality was one of life's little challenges for her.

Clea Margulies, leaning against the driver's door of a battered old Chevy truck, chuckled. "No, I think we're early."

Mary moved so she could see inside the truck, to where Clea's husband sat in the passenger seat. "Hello. How are you?" She wished she could remember his name.

"Pretty good," he answered, a warm smile lighting his face.

Clea wore trim khaki slacks and a loose camp shirt with leather sandals, and her wavy silvering hair was brushed back from her face. Clea was, Mary decided, still as attractive as she'd been as a young woman.

A few years older than Mary's eldest sister Elizabeth, Clea had grown up in the same Mount Zion Mennonite Church congregation that the Classen girls had, but she'd left upon her marriage and joined her husband's Presbyterian church. After returning to Bird-in-Hand a few months ago, Mary had recognized Clea in the grocery store, and they had become reacquainted not long after Secondhand Blessings had reopened. Clea had asked if they'd be interested in some furniture she wanted to sell.

"I'm eager to move this stuff." Clea was nursing an insulated cup of coffee, and she reached through the open truck window and set it on the dash. "I should have done it when our daughter moved out years ago. It's been cluttering up the corner of a spare bedroom."

"Sometimes it's easier to tell ourselves we'll get to it 'someday,'" Mary said, smiling.

"Well, someday's here sooner than I anticipated," Clea said, not returning the smile.

Mary felt bad for her. When they'd caught up a few weeks ago, Clea had confided that her husband, who had retired a year or two earlier after a long career in banking, had been diagnosed with dementia. Their comfortable newly retired lives were already changing significantly, although Mary would not have guessed, looking at him today, that there was anything wrong. "Can I help you unload?" she asked. Clea was selling what she had described as "a few small pieces of furniture."

"That would be great." Clea walked around to the back of the truck. "As I told you when I called, these are not good pieces. I sent a few things to auction, but they weren't interested in these."

"Martha has repaired and painted some things that turned out beautifully, and others we've simply sold as is," Mary assured her.

As Clea opened the tailgate of the truck, her husband called, "Want me to help with that?"

"We've got it, Leon," Clea told him. "Just stay there. I'll only be a minute."

Mary carefully removed a small, simple rocker. Beneath the scratches and dulled finish, its good lines and sturdy frame made her suspect it was Amish-made. "Oh, this is adorable."

Clea pulled out a small bedside table. "I bought these together at an estate sale years ago when our daughter was small," she said with a smile, hefting the table as Mary picked up the chair. "They are well-loved."

"Let's take them inside," Mary said. "I'll give you a receipt for them, and when Martha and Elizabeth arrive, we'll evaluate them, and I'll call you with an offer."

"Sounds good to me," Clea said. Mary set the rocker inside the shop door, and Clea did the same with the table. Mary would enlist her sisters' help to carry the items to the back room when they arrived.

The two women returned to the truck and unloaded a small desk and chair set and a little bookcase with carved flowers trailing across the top. Mary could almost see it with a soft pink wash for a little girl's room.

As Clea thanked her, pocketed a receipt, and drove away, Mary saw her sisters coming down the hill. Martha carried a box of baked goods, and Elizabeth had a satchel over her shoulder.

Waving to them, she called, "Martha, you're going to love this furniture Clea Margulies brought us. It's begging for your special touch."

Martha smiled. "I finished the last piece I was painting yesterday. Time for something new."

"Speaking of new," Elizabeth said, "Martha's got a treat for us. Remember Ruth Zook's delicious coffee cake recipe?"

Mary laughed. "Yes, although I certainly never got a look at it. Ruth guarded that recipe like it was the Hope Diamond." Ruth Zook and her husband, their former pastor, had retired to Florida a few months ago. Before she moved, Ruth had entrusted Martha with her secret coffee cake recipe.

"I made it this morning," Martha said. "It smells divine."

"It *is* divine," Mary said. "I may as well glue a couple of pieces on each thigh. I can't stay away from the stuff." She gestured to the furniture Clea had dropped off. "We need to move these pieces to the stockroom."

Martha chuckled. "Give us a minute to set up the cash drawer, and we both can help."

All three sisters entered the barn and spread out to begin their day. Within minutes, cars were pulling into the lot out front, and customers wandered through the aisles, browsing the newest items or looking for specific finds.

The miscellany on the tables in the center of the shop seemed to become disordered the fastest. After Mary finished "redding up," a phrase for tidying the house that she rarely heard anywhere outside Pennsylvania Dutch country, she turned toward the door, where Clea's furniture still sat. "I'm going to move those to the back," she called to Elizabeth.

Her sister waved. "I'll lend you a hand when I'm done here." She was completing a sale, while Martha was helping someone look for small appliances at the back of the store.

Mary headed for the door. Hefting the small end table Clea had given them, she turned with it—and gasped as the single drawer fell out with a loud clatter, and a plethora of papers spilled across the floor.

"Oh my!" Nancy VanSlyke, a frequent visitor who often consigned or sold things she'd found at garage sales, gasped and slapped a hand to her chest. She started forward and dropped to her knees as Mary set the table down and knelt also. "Here. Let me help you pick those up."

A man not far away bent and began to gather up sheets of paper that had scattered a bit farther, and another woman moved in to help also.

"There," Nancy said a moment later. "All cleaned up."

"Thanks, everyone." Mary smiled and shook her head. "That certainly raised my heart rate for the day."

The second woman chuckled. "Sure startled me." It was Peggy Hockensmith, a local hairdresser. Mary had never used Peggy's services, but she knew several people who did.

Turning, Mary extended her hand to the man who had given her the spilled papers. "I'm Mary Baxter. Thanks for your help."

"No problem." He gave her hand a firm shake. "Harold Brewerton." He held up a cellophane-wrapped piece of Martha's coffee cake. "I didn't come in to buy food, but I couldn't resist this. Right place at the right time, I suppose."

"Definitely," Mary said. "Thanks again, all of you."

Elizabeth hurried over, a plastic grocery bag extended. "Here. Put those in here."

"Don't toss them out," Mary warned, sliding the stack of envelopes, loose papers, and magazines she and the others had collected from the floor into the bag. "These are things that came out of Clea's end table. She must have forgotten to empty this drawer."

Elizabeth pulled out some of the papers and riffled through them. "Oh dear. Some of them look like recent invoices."

Mary blew out a breath. "She said these were unused pieces of furniture. Let me check to be sure she didn't leave anything else in the other drawers, and I'll give her a call."

Elizabeth nodded. "All right." She glanced back at the lovely oak counter that family friend Bill Richmond had made and given to them shortly after they'd opened. Two customers awaited. "Back to business," she murmured.

Mary followed her sister, where she placed the bag beneath the counter after writing Clea's name on it. Then she looked at the contact information she'd had Clea complete on the receipt and gave her a call.

"Hi, Clea," she said when her friend answered. "It's Mary at Secondhand Blessings. We found some mail and paperwork of yours in the end table you brought. Some of it looks recent."

"Oh dear," Clea said. "Thanks for calling. I'll run by and get it when I take Leon to the doctor later this morning."

As Mary hung up, Martha approached the counter. "I heard the clatter up here, but I missed the action," she said. "What happened?"

Mary explained the mishap, pointing to the bag beneath the counter. "Clea's things are here when she shows up. I guess you'll have to repair that drawer before you paint it. The bottom split when it fell."

Martha nodded. "All right."

"Hey Martha, have you heard about the bake-off Mount Zion Mennonite is doing to benefit Noah Beiler's family?" asked Nancy VanSlyke. After helping Mary pick up the papers, Nancy

262 | MYSTERIES of LANCASTER COUNTY

had purchased a piece of coffee cake and was nibbling as she and her friends Della, Linda, and Beverly waited to show the sisters what they'd found during their latest yard sale rounds.

Noah and Rebecca Beiler were a young couple in the local Amish community who had five children. Four had been diagnosed with a devastating genetic disorder and needed lifesaving treatments if they were to survive. Many churches in the area, Amish and Mennonite alike, were raising funds to help the family with medical expenses.

"Bake-off?" Martha looked thoughtful.

"Your Italian cream cake is to die for," Mary said. "That could be a winner."

"Or your caramel apple pie," Elizabeth put in.

"*This* is a winner, in my opinion," Nancy said. She held up the coffee cake. "It tastes just like Ruth Zook's, and she made the best coffee cake in town."

Martha chuckled. "It's Ruth's recipe. She gave it to me before she moved."

"Ruth's coffee cake is good," Linda Martin said, "but I think Essie Baldwin's might be better. She made it for our fellowship meeting last month, and I swear it melted in my mouth."

"I heard Essie is entering hers in the bake-off," Beverly Stout said. Her blue eyes twinkled. "Maybe you two should go head-to-head and decide once and for all who makes the best coffee cake."

"Maybe we should," Martha said. Mary was a little surprised by the determined glint that appeared in her sister's eye. "I'm pretty confident Ruth's is the best, but maybe I could tweak it a bit to punch it up a little."

"Now you've done it," Mary said to Beverly. "If Martha's-slash-Ruth's coffee cake doesn't win, she won't be fit to live with."

All the women laughed, even Martha. "But mine's going to win," she said, "so it's a moot point."

Shortly before noon Clea stepped into the shop. Mary, who was manning the register, waved at her. "Hi, Clea. I have your things right over here." As Clea drew close to the counter, Mary withdrew the bag from beneath it and handed it to her.

"Thank you so much." Clea took the grocery bag with a shake of her head. "I feel like an idiot. I had forgotten I stored some important things in that desk."

"It could happen to anyone," Mary reassured her.

"There are so many things running around in my head that I can't keep anything straight." Clea sighed. "I'm so worried about how expensive it's going to be to make this move from a house to a retirement cottage."

"Have you visited any senior living facilities and gotten cost estimates?" Mary asked. "I'm sure they vary widely."

"I've talked to several friends who know people who have purchased cottages in different places," Clea said. "No matter where we go, it's going to be costly." Her eyes filled. "It's hard to think of leaving our home. We bought this house specifically because there was a full bath on the main floor, and we'd be able to grow old in it. I figured when we were ancient, we could just live on one floor, but Leon's had trouble with his balance, so I set up a bedroom on the first floor last spring."

"Are you sure you can't stay there?"

Clea shook her head. "As his illness progresses, I'm not going to be able to care for him myself. I've heard about places where you can buy a cottage and be independent as long as possible and then start having help come in as needed. And then, eventually, if he needs to be moved into a facility that offers full nursing care, we would already be right there."

"I see," Mary said. "That sounds like a good plan."

"And I'd like to do it soon, so he gets used to the new place while he's still got some of his faculties." Clea sighed again. "We love our house. Dementia wasn't something either one of us ever thought would interrupt our plans."

"No one does," Mary said gently. "I'm so sorry. It's a terrible disease."

"Leon was a stamp collector," Clea said. "He used to spend hours poring over his stamps and searching out the next special one he hoped to find at auction or buy from another collector. Now he's struggling to remember the names of the stamps. Same with baseball. We followed the Orioles for years. I mentioned Cal Ripken the other day, and Leon said he hadn't seen him at church in a while."

Mary whipped a tissue from a box beneath the counter and came around to put an arm around Clea's shoulders and offer her the tissue. "If there is any way we can help, please let us know."

Clea blotted her eyes. "Thank you, but he's my husband, and I signed on for better or for worse. I really appreciate you looking at the furniture. It's possible I'll have some other things to consign as I get serious about going through our belongings. We aren't going to have very much room in a cottage."

"We'd be happy to take anything you want to send our way."

As Clea hurried out, still dabbing at tears, Mary's heart ached. What a difficult journey to undertake after so many years of marriage. When her own marriage had been intact, she had certainly never considered that something like dementia could ruin what were supposed to be Brian's and her golden years. Then she gave herself a mental shake. There would be no golden years of marriage for her, but she was finally beginning to be able to see a future for herself as an independent, single woman. A businesswoman, she corrected, looking around the thrift shop, where a satisfying number of customers browsed. She and her sisters were making their dream come true.

When a lull in shopping permitted, Mary and Elizabeth moved Clea's furniture to the back room, where Martha was eager to begin assessing it. "This is just adorable," Mary said, gently running her hands over the little bookshelf.

"It is," Elizabeth agreed. "I could imagine it in a child's room."

"It would be perfect, wouldn't it?" Mary asked. The telephone near the register rang, and she turned. "I'll get that."

Hurrying back to the counter, she reached for the handset. "Secondhand Blessings, this is Mary. How may I help you?"

"Mary! It's Clea." The woman's voice was filled with alarm. "Where's the rest of our stuff?"